Thanksgiving Horror Anthology

Copyright © Allisha McAdoo 2023

This book may not be reproduced or used in any manner without the publisher's express written permission except for brief quotations in a book review in the United States of America. The characters are purely fictitious. Any likeness to persons living or dead is coincidental.

First Printing, 2023

Cover created by Niyah M.

- Table of Contents
- Served cold by Kelly Barker
- Feast by Holly Horror
- The Pumpkin Pie Man by Jason Jones
- The Importance of Tradition by Christopher Besonen
- Barnyard blood by Ivan K Conway
- Thanksgiving at the Cooper's House by Wade Cox
- Uncle Stu's Thanksgiving turkey by Lance

Loot
- The Contributor by Chase Will
- When black Friday comes by Jack Presby
- Cranberry sauce by Jason Gehlert
- Have some turkey by Allisha McAdoo

Prologue

"Ho! Ho! Ho!"

"Nope! Back it up Santa. This is a Thanksgiving horror anthology. Wait your turn!"

I wanted to create an anthology that showcases Thanksgiving dinner stories. I feel like Thanksgiving is often overlooked. It goes from Halloween straight to Christmas. This anthology is designed to showcase Thanksgiving in a new light. Each story is twisted in its way, so I hope you enjoy it!

Served Cold

By Kelly Barker

Sophie was in the kitchen with her mum, trying to

open a jar of cranberry—whatever the hell it was. It looked like cherry jam to her and there was no way it was going anywhere near her roast dinner. She glared at her mum. "I just don't see the point of Thanksgiving. Or why we're doing it today, of all days."

"Because it's his tradition. That's why?"

Her mum was on husband number six or seven now, and this was the first one from overseas. His accent drove her up the wall, and she could not have been more thankful for her demanding psychopathy course at Oxford Brookes. She was studying it, hoping to one day have a career as a forensic psychologist. The fact she and her mum scored high on the psycho-spectrum gave her an advantage the other students in her class would never have.

She looked down at the defiant jar, then at her reddened hands. "Yeah, I know it's his tradition. But why are we doing it today?"

Sophie's mum snatched the jar from her. It popped open in an instant before she slammed it down on the worktop. "I underestimated this one. I can tell he has doubts about our marriage."

Her mum was a master manipulator, the only person she knew who would pass a lie detector with ease. There was no way husband number six or seven suspected a thing.

"You're being paranoid."

"Listen to me. Good looks provide a smoke screen." She circled her face with her finger. "And this smoke screen is fading. I simply don't have the allure I once had."

"He's in love with you and would do anything you asked. He moved from the States for you."

She tutted. "His love for me will last as long as there is attraction. That's how wealthy men operate. How many times do I need to remind you that love is not unconditional?"

Sophie had always wanted to ask her mum if she thought their love for one another was unconditional, but she already knew the answer. They needed each other and worked as a team to make money. Her mum needed her help leading future husbands into pretenses by playing the dutiful stepdaughter, and her tech skills to locate far wealthier men than the last. And her mum, quite literally, was her bank, paying her wages with inheritance or insurance money if and when she needed it.

The question rolled around in Sophie's mind again. Except for this time, she asked herself instead. No, their love was not unconditional. She wouldn't think twice about hanging around if her mum was a skint, fat slob. No chance. She had places to go—a world to dominate.

"Still, I don't see the point of Thanksgiving." Sophie heaved herself up to sit on the worktop.

"Think of it like Christmas without trees, presents, and… fuck, I don't know."

They both giggled before her mum shushed her. Then she heard the rattle of keys from behind the front door.

"He's back early. I haven't done it yet," Sophie said, glancing at a miniature corked jar filled with cream powder.

"It's fine. We can still do it. I'll tell him I think the bathroom tap upstairs is leaking and he'll no doubt go up to take a look. Then you can put it in. "

"I'm back," Husband number six or seven bellowed down the hallway.

Sophie put her hand over her ears, ground her teeth, then hopped off the worktop. The smile she often practiced in the mirror was in place, and she cleared her throat, attempting to clear the natural huskiness of her tone.

"In here, my darling." Her mum's tone was cashmere soft, and her smile was effortless, mastered over countless years of playing the loving wife. Only Sophie saw her authentic smile. It was sly, calculating, and yet powerful.

Husband number six or seven entered the kitchen with both arms outstretched and a bottle of red wine clutched in one hand. He wrapped his arms around my mum, and then put the bottle down.

"It smells incredible in here. You ladies have worked your magic. Are you sure you're not witches?"

Sophie didn't bother with her fake laugh. Instead, she used her sing-song voice to thank him.

"Well, hopefully, I have missed nothing out," her

mum said. "The turkey is in the oven. I've prepared the veg and the potatoes are about to go in."

"It looks fantastic, my love." He pulled two crystal glasses from the cupboard and then opened the bottle. "How are you getting on with the pumpkin pie?"

Sophie's mum cocked her head to the side. "Oh, no, I didn't think to make a pie. Although I must admit, I have never made one before. Do we have to have one?"

He filled the glasses, then handed one to her mum first, then her. Sophie didn't drink often, and especially not when she and her mum were executing a plan. However, one glass wouldn't hurt.

"It wouldn't be the same without one. You two ladies carry on, and I'll go to the store and get one."

Sophie sipped her wine. "I don't think our shops sell them—"

"Well, they might," her mum said, giving her a pointed stare. "We just weren't looking out for them, that's all."

"You're right," Sophie said, taking another sip.

Her mum leaned into him. "You have an hour or so before dinner is served. I hope you find one."

Before he kissed her mum's cheek goodbye, Sophie could have sworn she glimpsed a flash of disgust on his face before he concealed it with a smile.

Something didn't feel right, making Sophie take note. But her mind couldn't unravel the cause of concern fast enough. When she heard the front door close, she said, "Mum, did you notice something different about him?"

"I told you; he's starting to suspect something. That's why we're doing it today. A day when he'll be distracted by food, beer, and sports." She sipped her wine. "Now, pass me the ground phalloides. I'll mix it in with the cranberries."

"No, mum. The powder is cream. It will make the cranberries go pale pink. Mix it in with the mash. It will serve him right for wanting roasted and mashed potatoes on the same bloody plate."

They both smirked and then Sophie sobered. Her sharp mind had analyzed the lack of evidence and was on the cusp of seeing what most people would have missed.

"What is it?" her mum said.

"Didn't you notice how he only got two glasses out of the cupboard before asking where the pumpkin pie was? It's as if he already knew we didn't have one, then used it as an excuse to leave."

Her mum shrugged while mixing the powder into the mash, then sipped more wine. "It's normally just us two drinking together. Maybe he forgot. We needed him out of the way, anyway."

"No, he never forgets me." Feeling a sudden wave of dizziness, Sophie pinched her forehead. "And I've never seen him... look at you... with disgust before."

Her mum stumbled back from the worktop, then tripped backward. "I don't... feel right. I must have... inhaled the... phalloides power."

"You didn't. It's in... the wine," Sophie tried to say, sounding as breathless as her mum. Her legs buckled under her weight and the wine glass clutched in her hand became too heavy to hold.

Fear spiking her heart rate was short-lived, for she had never felt so tired—so weightless. When her head hit the tiled floor, she did not feel the pain that should have accompanied the impact.

* * *

Sophie felt a sharp pain in her neck before her eyes flew open, only to be greeted by a blurry mass of color. Her mind couldn't decipher her surroundings fast enough, making her skin prickle. She was sitting upright. That much she knew. And there was a familiar smell in the air. The aromas of cooked food sparked confusion, which sparked panic. Something cut into her wrist when she tried to rub her eyes.

"No. What's happening? Mum!" Her legs kicked out, to no avail.

"You're taped to a chair," husband number six or seven said. "From your wrists to your elbows, ankles to knees, and around your waist. Your mum is sitting opposite you, still out for the count."

"What? Why? Why are you doing this?" Her blurry

vision cleared enough to see that her forearms and the chair's arms were indeed wrapped in silver tape. Then she saw the outline of her mum, with her chin resting on her chest. The food which they had been preparing was cooked and laid out across the table.

"I think you know," he said.

"I don't. I don't." She tried to shuffle forwards, but the chair was too heavy—the best that money could buy, bought with husband number four's inheritance. "Untie me. I can't feel my hands."

"I believe you. They've gone pale blue."

Sophie eyed him to her left, sitting at the table as stoic as his tone was. From what she had learned from studying human emotions, she could tell he wasn't enjoying this. Which, in a way, was much worse. She noted how his eyes were unreadable. Unreadable meant unpredictable. Then he drummed his fingers over the arm of his chair, showing her he was calm and in control. Meaning, he was unlikely to negotiate.

"Just tell me what you want. Or what it is you're planning to do to us."

Without turning to look in her direction, he said, "I will, but first, I want you to know why I'm doing this."

"Because you found out about my mum's countless husbands and that she amassed millions from their deaths and not the trust fund she told you it came from."

"I've always known about that. Did I ever tell you about my Scottish ancestry?"

Scottish ancestry?

Within seconds the past and present clicked together like a puzzle, showing her an image that looked a lot like comeuppance. Now she knew for certain she wasn't getting out of this situation alive. Still, she would not beg for her life, nor would she die without giving him something to remember her by. "No, you haven't. I have something to tell you, though. Something that will rattle your cool demeanor."

"You know you're going to die, don't you? You see, I studied psychopathy too. It didn't amount to anything career-wise, but it taught me how to read people like a book. It's how I knew you two were behind my uncle's death."

"And I bet you're just dying to tell me how you worked it all out."

"It was at his funeral. I was a lot younger back then and had hung back in the treeline, unable to stand any closer in fear of breaking down in front of people. You were just a little girl back then and why I waited before striking. Turns out, the apple doesn't fall far from the tree, reminding me of the two-headed snake I once saw at Audubon Zoo in New Orleans."

When he mentioned she had just been a little girl, she thought she could argue her case by saying she didn't know any better, and blame everything on her mum. However, his last statement reinforced the rules of this game: no negotiation.

He scratched his chin. "What was it you wanted to tell me?"

"Husband number four was Scottish—"

"Is that how you refer to us? Husband number one, two, so on and so on."

"And you're sitting at the dining room table your beloved uncle paid for."

The desired effect fell flat when his lips curved into a half smile. "Ironic then, is it? That you will die at his table."

She ground her teeth in response.

"You're right, though. He was my beloved uncle. He enjoyed telling me stories when I was a child about the Loch Ness Monster and took pride in teaching me about our history, mythology, and legends. You and your mother destroyed a good man. A man that would have done anything for anyone." He stirred the now cold mashed potatoes with a gloved hand, then sighed. "Didn't you have any love for him at all? Didn't you feel any pity for him after your mom drugged him, then slit his wrists in the bath to make it look like a suicide?"

Sophie refused to answer him, not wanting to give him closure. "Just get to the point and do what it is you're going to do to us."

He shrugged. "I've already done it."

Sophie's brows furrowed. "Done what? What have you done?"

"What I set out to do all along."

Her mum groaned but was still too weak to lift her head.

"You'll never get away with it."

"I already have. Right now, as we speak, I'm spending Thanksgiving with my mom in Maine. You see, money buys more than just designer shoes and jewels; it buys private planes, airfields, forged papers, etc."

Her scream scratched the inside of her throat.

"What's happening?" her mum said, straining against the restraints. "What are you doing?"

This time, when he spoke, he made eye contact with both of them. "You're both taped to the chairs in a way that prevents you from escaping. No one will hear you scream thanks to your late husbands, who paid for this fortress on private land surrounded by trees. And the best part is that while you're dying of dehydration and starvation, you'll have this beautiful banquet sitting right in front of you. Enjoy."

With that, Husband number six or seven, known to his loved ones as Duncan, stood, straightened his chair, and then walked away to the chorus of screams.

The End

About the author: Kelly Barker was born in Oxford and now lives in Witney with her husband and dog, Lana. She has been a barber for over twenty years and loves her job. However, reading and writing is her passion—a passion handed down to her by her great-grandmother, Isobel O'Leary. **www.kellybarker.org** Also by Kelly Barker The Inner Temple, Even the Gods Fear It, Necromantia, Breaking His House Rules

Feast
By Holly Horror

Sitting outside in the cold autumn evening, the sun beginning to touch the horizon, I watch as the leaves fall to the ground letting us know that winter is near. I pick up a golden maple leaf and crumple it in my fist.

My head shoots up as the sound of a vehicle approaches. When the vehicle is in sight, I recognize the shiny black Bentley as it comes around our wrap-around driveway. When it parks, the back door swings open and Mrs. Vanderbilt steps out. She looks every bit the Norwegian beauty that she is, with the help of procedures, of course. She wraps her mink fur coat tight around her body and turns to face me.

"Oh, Austin," she says in a high-pitched tone as she walks over to where I stand under the maple tree. She places her hands on either side of my face, looking me in the eyes no doubt spotting the dread in them.

"I'm so sorry to hear about your mother, dear. Any word from her or the police yet?"

Shaking my head, all I can muster up is a simple, "No."

My mother has been missing since yesterday morning. She had left for the salon and never returned. The last couple of nights they had gotten into rather nasty arguments. Although they would sometimes fight, they adored each other.

The Vanderbilt's have been a friend of our family for many years. Their son, Bartholomew, and I had grown up together. There are even pictures of us playing together in our diapers. A few years back when we were fifteen, Bartholomew had started getting into trouble at the private school we attended. He started to partake in drugs, sleeping with random girls, and getting into fights. The

Vanderbilt name was constantly in the media, bringing shame to their family. Around this time two years ago, Bartholomew disappeared. Freya and Michael Vanderbilt claim to have sent him off to boarding school. I've asked for the name of the school so I can write to him, but they refuse to tell anyone where he has gone. Just that he's across the pond.

Bartholomew is eighteen now, a legal adult. He should have come back home by now. It seems every year around Thanksgiving someone in town goes missing, and I can't help but think the Vanderbilt's have something to do with these mysterious disappearances.

Freya gives my cheek a soft pat, then turns to walk up the steps to our home, me following right behind her.

"Edgar! Edgar, dear," she shouts from the foyer. My father's heavy footsteps can be heard crossing the balcony overlooking the foyer and then beginning to descend the staircase. When he reaches us, his eyes are red and glossy, his pain mirroring my own.

"Oh, Edgar, darling," Freya says walking up to my father and placing her hands on his forearms.

"There's still no word on Eloise?"

"No, I'm afraid not," he replies. "The police are continuing their search. They believe she had just taken some time away from us having been arguing lately. But she hasn't used any of her cards and hasn't bought a plane or bus ticket. Her car hasn't been seen on any cameras. It's like she just...disappeared."

He takes a deep breath, shoulders sagging. Freya removes her coat, places it on the rack, and grabs my father by the hand. I sneer behind her back at the contact. Yes, they're long-time friends and although she puts on a proper and polite facade, I feel there's a snake beneath her surgically enhanced skin.

Freya continues to pull my father along into the kitchen. She reaches inside the wine cooler and brings out an expensive bottle of vintage red. Popping the cork, she fills two glasses. Handing my father one, she takes a long sip from her own.

"Edgar, I do apologize that you are going through this. I wish there were more I could do. Eloise is my friend and I am worried about her."

My father just nods his head, taking a shuddering breath. He's doing everything he can to hold himself together. I step to my father's side and place my hand on his shoulder, giving a squeeze for comfort. He reaches up and gives my hand a gentle pat.

Freya continues, "Maybe she did just take some time off. She could've had a friend pick her up. What about her friend Margaret? I recall her saying something about her coming for a visit soon.

But what about another man?"

My father's body stiffens and I'm getting pissed. I argue that my mother would never do such a thing to my father.

Getting up, Freya places her wine glass into the sink and turns to me.

"I believe you are correct Austin. I don't think Eloise would do such a thing. But she could be off with Margaret. Just taking a breather after the last few days and with Thanksgiving a couple of days away." She turns to my father. "Either way, Edgar, Michael, and I would love it if you still came to our annual Thanksgiving feast. I hope Eloise shows up before then, but if not it would be good for you and Austin to get out of the house."

Curious of her response, I ask, "Will Bartholomew be coming this year? "

Freya pins her eyes on me, a sinister look flashes in her pretty blues for a split second. She crosses her arms over her chest, a look of defiance.

"It's doubtful," she scoffs. "That boy won't return my calls or letters. It's like he fell off the face of the planet."

Something in her tone chills me to the marrow.

"We'll still come," my father says, downing the rest of his wine. "If Eloise hasn't returned by then, I could use the comfort of friends."

"Marvelous," Freya shouts, clapping her hands, and walks in the direction of the foyer, my father and I following behind her.

"The Beumont's and the Romero's will be joining us as well. I'm making my famous pork loin in a rich red wine sauce along with an Apple Cider brined turkey." My father retrieves her coat and helps her put it on.

"It sounds lovely, Freya. We'll see you on Thursday," he says and opens the front door. Freya leans in to give my father a quick kiss on the cheek, then she does the same to me. She looks at me, then to my father.

"If you need anything, please don't hesitate to call Michael or me. We'd love to help any way that we can."

My father gives her another sad nod. I open my mouth to thank her, but before I can, she's out the door. My father shuts the door and without a word, makes his way back up the stairs where he's spent most of the last thirty-two hours.

I don't want to attend Vanderbilt's annual Thanksgiving feast, but I'm curious about Bartholomew's disappearance. I want to do some digging around while I'm there. The Vanderbilt's always seemed nice enough, but I have always gotten an odd, uncomfortable feeling about them, even when I was a young boy.

It's Thanksgiving morning. I walk downstairs and begin to prepare breakfast for my father and I. Cracking the eggs into the skillet, I jump at the sound of my father's shouts from inside his study and drop an egg on the floor.

"I don't give a fuck if it's Thanksgiving. I wouldn't give a fuck if you were on your God damned deathbed! Do your job and find my wife! I'm paying you more than what is required!" I stand there staring at the broken shell and yolk splattered across the marble tile. We still haven't gotten any news about my mother. The detective has reached out to her friend, Margaret, as well as anyone else in her call log. No one has seen, nor spoken to her. There were no other calls or messages aside from my father, Freya, the salon, and I. We've hit another dead end.

I see water dropping down to the marble mixing with the splattered egg yolk. I realize that I'm crying. I'm not an emotional person, but not knowing what has happened to my mother has taken its toll on me. On us. It's driven a wedge between my father and me. He barely leaves his bedroom or study. I haven't seen him eat since her disappearance. It worries me. My father finishes his phone call and I hear his footsteps coming down the hall. I stand up, quickly wipe away my tears, and clean the mess on the floor before he sees me. I have to remain strong for him.

I continue cooking a breakfast of eggs, thick-cut bacon, and toast. I cut up fresh fruits and add them to the plate. I place the plates down on the table as well as a pitcher of orange juice just as my father enters the kitchen.

"Good morning, dad," I say. His only response is a grunt, but he at least sits at the table and starts poking his breakfast with his fork.

Sitting down across from him, I pour myself a glass of juice. We eat together in silence which seems to go on forever. My father has barely eaten his breakfast when he sets down his napkin. He stares at me for a moment and I take the time to study his features. His face is gaunt. He has dark bags under his eyes and his normally chocolate-colored eyes look black surrounded by redness.

He breaks his stare and clears his throat.

"I just got off the phone with Detective Peterson. He thinks we should start thinking about the worst-case scenario."

I drop my fork and give my father a confused look. "What the hell does that mean? "

"The detective says that he believes she's gone, son. Dead. There's been no sign of her. No tips have come in. Anyone we could think of who knows her has not seen nor heard from her. She hasn't used her phone and there's no way to track her location from her phone. She hasn't written any checks or used her cards. They cannot find her car anywhere."

My eyes fill with tears and they quickly spill out, rolling down my cheeks. My body begins to tremble. I can no longer hold my emotions in. I fell apart with my father.

"Mom would never just abandon us. She would never just up and leave us like that," I cry out, knowing that the detective is probably right.

My father rushes to my side and wraps me in an embrace. I cry on his shoulder like I'm a little boy again except now his embrace is weaker. He's gotten so weak these last several days.

"I know, son. I know. I know," he repeats. I feel his tears mix with mine.
"Maybe we should just stay home tonight and order Chinese. Maybe it's best to avoid the Vanderbilt's at the moment."
I pull back and wipe my tears away onto my sleeve. I don't want to miss out on Thanksgiving. It'll be the perfect time for me to dig around while the Vanderbilt's are busy entertaining guests.
"No, Dad. We should still go. We attend every year. We can use the distraction and a good meal.
Don't take this the wrong way, but you look like hell."
At that, I'm rewarded with a warm laugh. He kisses the top of my head and grabs his coffee mug.
"Then we will attend. I have some work to get caught up on before we head out."

I look at myself in the full-length mirror inside of my walk-in closet. I held up a few ties trying to decide which one to wear this evening. I decided to forgo the suit and go with a simple pair of jeans and a Henley sweater. I run the comb over my dark blond hair. Making my way downstairs, I see my father pull his Mercedes up to the front door. It's gotten cold enough to where I can see my breath.
I jumped into the passenger side and quickly shut the door. Driving off, we head over to the Vanderbilt's. The drive is only ten minutes before reaching their gate. The security guard recognizes my father's car and allows us to pull through.

Pulling up to Vanderbilt's abysmally over-priced modern structure of a mansion, my father parks the car and we head up the steps to the large porch adorned with pumpkins, scarecrows, and wreaths made from fall foliage. Before we ring the bell I grab my father's hand squeezing it. He looks at me and gives me one of those sad smiles I've seen far too many times lately.

I ring the doorbell and Helga, one of the Vanderbilt's hired help, opens the door. She greets us with a smile and then ushers us into the warm house. We follow her to one of the sitting rooms. Mr. Vanderbilt, Mr. Romero, and Mr. Beumont sit on black leather couches all dressed to the nines in similar tailored suits, sipping cognac and smoking Cuban cigars. Michael Vanderbilt sees us and stands to greet us, offering us his hand to shake. Pulling my father in, he throws his arm around his shoulder in a gentlemanly hug. No words are needed. The anguish on my father's face speaks volumes. He hands us each a cigar which I kindly decline, but my father grabs one and lights it up. He orders another helper to pour us a drink and although I begin to decline, I decide to say fuck it, I've had a rough enough week.

My father looks like he wants to protest considering I'm only 18, but must see the sadness in my eyes and instead gives a slight nod of permission.

In the other room, I hear the faint voices of women and the rattle of China and silverware being sat down on the dining table. The smell of the delectable meal is appealing to my senses.

Freya peeks into the sitting room. I watch her from the corner of my eye. Her smile is disturbing.

"Gentleman," she calls out. "Come. The feast is ready."

We stand and follow Mrs. Vanderbilt into the large dining room. Approaching our places at the table, everyone compliments Freya on her festive decor. Mrs. Romero and Mrs. Beumont have already taken their place. There are candles lit inside little autumn wreaths along the top of the mahogany table. Thick garlands are strung around the chandelier, atop the floor-to-ceiling windows, and across the fireplace mantle. Fine China is set with name cards on top of our assigned seats, as well as crystal glasses and silver cutlery. A large turkey rests upon a silver platter. Next to it is another dish with tenderloin in a bold red sauce. There are mashed potatoes, crab stuffed pumpkin, sausages, green bean casserole, roasted rosemary carrots, garden salad, corn pudding, fresh bread, and so many desserts.

We say our prayers which, of course, mention my mother and Bartholomew. After the toast, the dishes are being passed around and we scoop a little of each onto our plates. Just when everyone had been served and started eating, I decided now was the time.

"Excuse me for a moment, but I must visit the washroom," I say as I stand. Freya pats her mouth with her napkin and points behind me.

"Of course, dear. You know the way."

I slip away down the hall to the back staircase that leads closer to Bartholomew's bedroom than the main stairs. Reaching the second floor, I peek around the corner making sure none of the help is around. When I see the coast is clear I walk with steady steps to Bartholomew's door. Quietly opening it, I slip inside and turn on the lights. The room no longer holds the warmth it once did, although it looks the same as it did before he disappeared. The room feels like it holds secrets. I rummage through his bureau and look under his bed. Something feels off.

I come to his closet door and flip the light switch. To my surprise, all his luggage is still there. His closet and drawers are full as if he left with nothing. I exit and check his en-suite bathroom, then his nightstand. Opening the drawer my heart drops. There, right fucking there is Bartholomew's wallet, passport, and phone in the top drawer.

Hearing footsteps down the hall, I quickly place the items back inside and walk to the door. I listen as the footsteps walk by and down the steps. Once I know they're gone, I slip out of the bedroom shutting the door behind me. I think for a minute. Where could he be? All his things are here. He would need his identification and passport to go overseas.

I decided to return to the dining room. When I take my place at the table all eyes are on me.

"Feeling okay, son?" my father asks.

"Yeah. Just feeling a little nauseous." It isn't a lie. I have this feeling of foreboding. There's something the Vanderbilt's are hiding.

"Austin, you must eat." Michael motions his arm at the meal in front of us. "The food is fantastic. I'm sure you haven't eaten much. You need your strength." Freya nods, agreeing with her husband.

"It's true, dear. You and your father don't look well. Try my famous pork."

"It's amazing pork, Freya," Mrs. Beumont says in her thick, French accent. The table all grumble their agreement with full mouths.

I turn to my father who has devoured all the meat and is currently shoveling potatoes in his mouth. The feeling of unease lessens a bit at the sight of my father eating. I grab my fork and knife, cut off a piece of pork, and take a bite. It's delicious. I continue eating, the sound of conversation around me a blur. I try to think of my next move. Where I could look next? The basement! The basement is dark and damp, but part of it had been converted into a man cave. He could be down there. I focus back on the conversation around me as Mrs. Romero brags about her children's success to the Vanderbilt's. Mr. and Mrs. Beumont talked to my father about their recent family trip to Fiji for their son's wedding. I look down at my plate, surprised that I've cleared it. Mrs. Vanderbilt doesn't do much around here, but she loves to cook and she's damn good at it.

I wait until the dinner plates are taken away and dessert is being served before I excuse myself again.

"Austin. Are you okay?" Mrs. Beumont asks. She looks concerned. This is the second time I've excused myself tonight. I hope I'm not raising suspicion.

"I'm fine, Mrs. Beumont, thank you. I've eaten too much. I feel I've overdone it." The men laugh. "Be sure to use the room spray when you're finished, will ya," Mr. Vanderbilt calls out. Freya slaps her husband on the arm. "Michael! That is not appropriate dinner talk amongst guests!" I shake my head at them and head out of the room. This time I take another hallway that leads to the other side of the kitchen close to the basement door. From here, I won't be spotted from the dining room. Opening the door, I walk down the wooden steps. I reach the bottom unsure of where to start in this enormous space. The basement is separated by three rooms. The first is storage. When you walk straight ahead there's a door leading to another room. I never liked that one. It always reminded me of a dungeon. To my right is the door that leads into the converted area. It's a large room with a TV, pool table, bar, a small kitchen and bathroom. Many times Bartholomew and I would sneak down here and try the different liquors on the shelf behind the bar. This is Mr. Vanderbilt's man cave. I decided to check inside there first. Opening the door I walk inside turn on the light and search the space. Nothing. I walk back out and shut the door. Searching the storage area and coming up spotting nothing, my eyes look up at the last door. Hands on my hips I let out an exasperated breath. I don't want to find out what's behind door number three. My feet move on their own accord anyway. As I get closer to it I notice a faint metallic smell. Reaching for the knob I swing it open. The room is pitch black, but the smell, fuck, the smell is horrid. It reminds me of the dead deer Bartholomew and I found out in the woods behind his house. Feeling along the wall on my right I flip on the light switch and my body freezes in terror. The sight in front of me is a thing of nightmares. Something I thought I'd only see in horror movies.

Large hooks hang from the rafters. A butchered body hangs from one of them. The head missing. Body trembling, I manage to walk over to it. It's female, but her breasts have been removed, as well as all the innards. The chest cavity is void of organs. All the meat from her legs and abdomen has been removed, too. There's a drain in the center of the concrete floor with rivers of blood flowing into it. I turn to the side as burning vomit rises. This body is fresh! These sick fucks did not serve us humans for Thanksgiving. I look around the room and spot a table against the wall holding bloodied tools. Next to it is a large freezer. My heart races. Although everything in me is screaming for me not to open that freezer door, I do anyway. A blood-curdling scream escapes past my lips and I stumble back falling on my ass. "Mom?" There in the freezer staring back at me are the heads of my mother and Bartholomew. I jump to my feet and begin to run. Slipping in blood, I collide into the empty chest cavity on the hook and fall to my ass again. I turn to the side as more vomit makes its way up my throat, expelling my stomach's contents once again. Realization hits me that the body hanging from the hook is my mother. Trying to stand I stumble, my hands reaching out to the body to catch myself from falling. Turning toward the door, I see a shadow blocking my exit.

Mrs. Vanderbilt comes into view as she walks through the door. Her face twisted in a hateful look. She walks up to me and looks over at my mother's body.

"Don't worry, dear. We kept her alive up until last night. The meat tastes better fresh."

"You did this? You killed my mother and your son?"

She shrugs her shoulders and steps closer to me. I step back, my back touching my mother's corpse.

"Bartholomew was a problem. His behavior was putting too much attention on our family. The police had brought him home several times. I couldn't allow that to continue and have them find out our secrets. Instead, I killed him and served him to you all that Thanksgiving." "Your secrets?" I laugh, but there's no humor in it. Just fear. "You kill people and serve them to guests as a holiday feast!"

"No, Austin. Not just the holidays. What do you think are in the casseroles and meat pies I would bring over, hmmm? As for your mother, our friendship started to drift apart. She seemed to no longer trust me. And, with us needing a body for the feast, I decided to get rid of her as well."

"You're fucking sick," I spit out. I rush toward her just as I hear my father's voice coming into the basement.

"Austin, are you down here?"

"Dad, run! They killed mom!"

My father enters the room, face-paling when he spots the body hanging from the hook. His face turns to the freezer seeing the decapitated heads.

"What? No!" He collapses on the ground screaming my mother's name. Looking up at Freya, he gets back to his feet and in seconds has Freya's neck in his grasp, squeezing. Her face turned red.

"What did you do, Freya? Why?"

She can't say anything, but she smiles that sinister smile and looks over my father's shoulder. I follow her line of sight just as Michael comes up behind my father, a hammer in his hand, and swings it down on my father's head with a sickening crunch. Blood trails down his forehead and he releases Freya's throat, his body dropping to the ground.

Sickened, I rush over to Mr. Vanderbilt. Fist balled, I landed a punch to his jaw at the same time something hard hit my back. Sharp pain jolts my body and I crumple to the floor. I look up to see

Freya, a large pipe in her hands. She holds the pipe like a golf club and swings it at my head. I hear the crack before I feel the pain. Everything around me is fading into blackness.

I'm at the table in my home. My mother sits on one end of the dining table, my father on the other. There's turkey in the center as well as many other dishes. My mother and father stare at each other lovingly as they eat their meal. I smile. They seemed to have moved past whatever they had been arguing about. I lift my fork to my mouth and take a bite of the turkey. My food is almost gone when I realize the turkey tastes wrong. It doesn't taste like turkey, but pork. I look down at my plate to see a chunk of raw, bloodied meat. I start gagging. My eyes look over the table again but my parents disappear. I try to say something but my mouth won't open, like it's being held shut while it's full of the meat.
"Swallow it, Austin," I hear a stern voice say, but it doesn't come from my parents, though it sounds familiar. Mrs. Vanderbilt?
Visions of my mother's fileted body hanging on a hook, her and Bartholomew's head in a freezer have my eyes popping open.
Freya's crimson-splattered face comes into view.
"There you are. You must finish your feast."
She steps aside and I look around the table. My eyes were still blurry but I could make out the faces of my mother and father frozen in an eternal scream.

"Fuucck," I shout and try to stand but the pain radiates down my spine. I struggle to move my arms and legs. They're bound to my chair.

I glance at the Vanderbilt's. Michael is using a carving knife and cutting away pieces of my father's cheek. Freya stands in front of me, a fork held out. I look at my plate and up at the utensil. She'd force-fed me while I was unconscious. Struggling in my binds, I start shouting for help.

Freya laughs, sounding every bit the psycho bitch she is.

" Oh, stop it. Everyone left after I told them you and your father weren't feeling well. Don't worry, though. I've sent them away with a tray filled with pieces of your mother."

She squats down before me, forcing me to look at her, and shoves the fork inside my mouth. I spit the flesh into her face. She grabs her napkin to clear it away.

"What's wrong, Austin? Don't like the taste of your mother's cunt," Mr. Vanderbilt says. He laughs at himself and brings a fork full of my father's cheek to his mouth.

Thrashing in my chair, I fight and scream curses their way. Michael walks over and shoves a forkful of my father between my lips. I try to spit it out again, but he clamps his paw over my mouth and pinches my nose shut, forcing me to swallow. When he kneels in front of me, I take the opportunity to head-butt him. He stumbles back, catching himself on the table. Reaching behind him, he grabs hold of my mother's head and throws it into my face. It falls onto my lap.

Her lifeless eyes look up at me. Panicking, I fall backward.

"ENOUGH," Freya shouts. Standing over me, she points a bloody finger in my face.

"You will be served next. Come now. Time to chain you in the basement until Christmas. You'll at least have the company of Bartholomew and your parents."

Michael drags my chair to the basement door, pushing me down the steps. I land at the bottom, the chair shattered around me, my arm feeling broken. Freya and Michael lift me by each arm and pull me to the back room. Attaching a shackle around my ankle that's mounted to the concrete wall, they toss the heads of my mother and father inside.

"Sleep tight," Freya whispers. Michael turns off the light as they both exit, leaving me in darkness with the ghosts of my loved ones. I start to scream and beg but my calls go unanswered. I can hear the door being locked from the outside. I continue screaming until my throat is raw and my voice is gone. I try to pry my foot out of the restraints causing myself to bleed. Defeated, I fell to the floor. I feel my mother's head next to me and start to gently stroke her hair with my fingers using my uninjured arm. There's no escape. In a month, I'll become a meal for Christmas. Coming to terms with my fate, I close my swollen eyes and wait

until December.
The End

About the author: Holly Horror is a sleep-deprived, hangry little demon, wife, mother of four, quite possibly part potato, and a mediocre writer. New to the indie horror scene, her first story —"Cursed Silver"— was published in the Cursed Items Anthology in April 2023. Holly also had a poem published under her real name at fifteen years old in Celebration of Young Readers, Florida edition, in 2000. Holly enjoys adventure and often spends time outdoors hiking, kayaking, fishing, or just tending to her yard. She also enjoys reading (of course), writing, painting, puzzles, Legos, and spending time with her family of five other humans, her Rottweiler Rollo, two yellow Lab pups named Bo and Jethro, Chaos the cat, and prairie dogs Bucky and Starla. She despises pickles and loves pizza. And whiskey. Maybe pizza dipped in whiskey? That should be a thing. And she will not do anything for a Klondike bar, so don't ask.

The Pumpkin Pie Man

By

Jason Jones

A few days before the Thanksgiving holiday in November of 1972, a crisp autumn breeze caressed the little town of Whispering Woods when the Pumpkin Pie man, as he would be known by everyone as the Thanksgiving holiday came to a close, drove through it, his little white panel truck trudging along the stretch of road that headed into the sleepy town. He threw an occasional smile and wave of the hand as he went down Cherry Street. Most of the kids were out of school for the week and many were out and about, riding their bikes and playing at the local playground. The Pumpkin Pie man stopped near a cul-de-sac near the Jenkins place on Waverly Road. The playground was just across the way. He waved his hand and called out of the driver's side window.

"Hey!" He said. Some of the children looked his way and stared. They'd never seen a car or truck for that matter that had a piece of pumpkin pie painted on the side of it with a dollop of whipped cream on top. A freakish, smiling, cartoon character held it in its hand with the words "It's Good!" hovering above in a word balloon. Just right above the word balloon, were the words, The Peddler's Pie Shop and Eatery in black lettering. He opened the truck door and climbed out. A few kids had already made their way towards him. He smiled.

"Hey boys and girls, my name is Tom Wilson and I have a question for you!" He licked his lips and moved his eyes from side to side, observing his audience. "Do you think any of your parents would like a delicious pumpkin pie to go along with their Thanksgiving meal?" Some of the children looked at each other and shrugged their shoulders. He knew this was going to be a long day. He needed to make a quota to get his holiday bonus. He continued.

"I not only have pumpkin but I have cherry, apple, blueberry, blackberry, I've got so many. A huge list!"

"My mom makes our pies." One of the children, Roy Childers yelled from the back of the small crowd that had gathered. Little heads began to nod in agreement.

"I'm sure she does, my little man, and I'll bet they're the best along this block but wouldn't you want to see your mom enjoying something that perhaps she didn't have to slave over and make? You know, give her a rest on this holiday. She'll probably be doing a ton of cooking anyway for your family, am I right?" he asked as he gave a hard pat on the side of his truck. Roy shook his head and said, "Maybe." It did make sense to his ten-year-old brain.

"Sure she would. Now, would you kids want to do a guy a favor and perhaps tell your moms and dads about me? I'll be around all day going up and down this street as well as throughout some other neighborhoods." He grinned as little smiles formed on the kids' faces. The Pumpkin Pie man got into his truck as many of the children made their way back to the swingsets and merry-go-rounds ends. He turned the ignition and started to drive down the block towards another area of town. He looked into the rearview mirror, the children growing smaller in the distance. He straightened up his black bow tie and adjusted in his seat, unbuttoning his white milkman-style suit jacket. He pulled out a cigar from his shirt pocket, swirling the tip around in his mouth.

Yes, it was going to be a long day, He thought, but a good one.

***

Roy Childers ran into the house, out of breath, and almost slammed into his grandmother, Josephine, who was visiting for the holiday from Cleveland. She happened to turn around just as Roy ran past her, trying to get to his mom, Marjorie, who was doing some early prep work for Thanksgiving.

"Hey, Mom!" Roy exclaimed. Although there was a definite chill in the autumn air, his forehead was wet with sweat and rightfully so as he had run all the way from the playground.

"Calm down, son. What's going on? Something wrong?" She wiped her hands on a kitchen towel and ran a hand through her son's hair. Roy finally began to settle down.

"No, nothing's wrong. There was a Pumpkin Pie man at the playground who was selling all kinds of pies!" He said.

"Pumpkin Pie man?... pies?" His mom asked.

"Yeah, you know the kind you eat." Roy rolled his eyes. He hoped his mom wouldn't see that. "The man wanted us to let you know." Roy continued. "I could take some of my allowance and buy one, that way you wouldn't have to slave over a stove and make one. Wouldn't you like that?"

His mom laughed, "That's awful sweet of you, Roy, but you know I always make my own desserts. You always like them more than anyone."

"Did someone say desserts?" Stanley Childers walked through the front door from the garage, his hands dirty from working on an engine block.

"You're not getting anything with those nasty hands of yours." Marjorie chortled. Stanley strolled up to his wife, pretending to rub his hands all over her, and quickly planted a kiss on her cheek, his lips were dry and weather-beaten. She wiped her face furiously with her hand. He chuckled as he went into the bathroom.

Marjorie turned her attention from her idiotic husband to her son, "So as I was saying, it's homemade from here on out. Ok, partner? Why don't you go back outside and play?"

"Okay." Roy looked defeated as he made his way towards the front door. But soon his dismay turned to pleasure as Jay Plymouth and Randy

Gillman rode up to his front steps and asked if he wanted to ride bikes. As they made their way across Cherry Street towards Fletcher Avenue, they passed the Whispering Woods Cemetery and up the street from there, a white panel truck sat, its driver taking long drags from a cigar.

***

Wednesday, November 22nd.

On the morning before Thanksgiving, with much of the prep work done, Marjorie sat down and reached for the Whispering Woods Reporter that lay in front of her on the coffee table. She unrolled it and quickly noticed the front page headline...

Family of Four Dead at 112 Waverly Road.

"That's just a few blocks over," Marjorie said, her flesh prickling beneath her bathroom robe. She jumped as the telephone rang in the kitchen.

"Hello," Marjorie said. Janice Bakely was on the other end.

"Did you see the paper this morning?" Janice said, frantically.

"I just saw it. It has to be the Jenkins family."

Janice continued, "I drove past there this morning on my way to the A&P and yeah, it was them. The police have the whole area sectioned off with crime scene tape, you know that yellow stuff they always use on those detective shows?"

Marjorie was dumbfounded. The whole reason for moving to Whispering Woods was to get away from the hustle and bustle of the big city and perhaps give Roy a normal childhood in a crime-free area. Murder in a small town? She knew it could happen, but why? And why the Jenkins family? She felt a hand on her shoulder. It was Stanley.

"Janice, I need to go, I need to talk to my husband." Marjorie hung up the phone in the cradle and turned toward him. She was trembling.

"What's wrong?" Stanley asked, groggily.

"You need to look at the paper." She said, her eyes fighting back tears.

***

"I just can't believe it," Stanley said as he clenched the paper tightly, slightly shaking.

The paper went on to identify the victims as forty-year-old, Tom Jenkins, thirty-five old, Samantha Jenkins, and twelve-year-old, Rachel Jenkins. Stanley had worked with Tom for the past ten years.

"Perhaps we should cancel Thanksgiving dinner tomorrow?" Marjorie said, her arms folded in front of her chest to gain some warmth. She suddenly felt a chill on her skin. Stanley put down the paper and walked toward his wife, putting his arms around her.

"No, let's celebrate tomorrow anyway. The police probably have this under control. We need to be vigilant though. We don't know who's out there. Where's Roy?" Stanley asked as he headed towards the bedroom to put on some clothes.

"I let him stay over at the Gillmans' last night. I'm sure he'll be ok." Marjorie looked out of the kitchen window at some of the homes on her street, she thought about the worst possible scenario of a killer on the loose. She shuddered.

While Stanley and Marjorie were trying to make

sense of what had happened, Roy Childers and Randy Gillman raced down Waverly Road towards the Jenkins place. They saw the crime scene tape and hit the brakes. Down the street, not too far from them and within hearing distance, a white panel truck sat. Roy glanced over his shoulder and saw it.

"Hey, it's The Pumpkin Pie guy," Randy said. They both took off on their bikes towards him. He waved at them, his eyes covered with dark sunglasses. The sky was overcast.

"Hey boys!" He called out to them. "Having fun?" The Pumpkin Pie man stared intensely at the Jenkins house.

"Tom Wilson, right?" Roy asked.

"You remembered. Good boy."

"Have you sold any pies yet?" Roy asked. He wondered why Tom was wearing sunglasses.

"Not a lick! Have you talked to your mom and dad about it?" He asked, lighting a cigar. As he flicked a matchstick and held the flame up to the cigar, Roy couldn't help but notice a strange flash beneath the sunglasses as if his eyes were milky.

"I did." Roy responded, "But mom said she was making everything for tomorrow's dinner, even the dessert."

"Ah, ok. I really gotta sell these pies, boys, they're gonna go bad if I don't." He looked toward the windshield at the Jenkins' house, his grip on the steering wheel, tightening. He clenched his teeth together, biting his cheek. He could taste blood.

"I'm sorry, Mr. Wilson," Roy said.

"So am I, Roy, so. . .am... .I. It's a shame." Tom Wilson said. "Hey, I got an idea. I could come by your house later today and ask your mom myself. How does that sound?" He grinned a smile that made both boys fidget on their bicycle seats.

"You can try, I guess," Roy said to the delight of the panel truck driver.

"You live around here?" Tom asked.

"See the playground over there? I live three houses down from it." Roy said, pointing and waving cigar smoke away from his face. The driver nodded his head in acknowledgment. He turned the ignition.

"Well boys, I gotta run. I'll see you, Mr. Roy, and your parents pretty soon. Oh, and it'd probably be a good idea not to tell your parents I'm coming by. If they know then I'll get the door slammed in my face. That's already happened this week." He laughed a hearty laugh and drove away. The boys made a trek towards the playground.

***

Wednesday, November 22nd: 2:45 p.m.

A knock on the door woke up Stanley Childers from a well-deserved nap. He'd worked most of the week and would only get two days off for the holiday. He had grumbled about it to his boss but his rant had fallen on deaf ears. He approached the front door and opened it. A man in sunglasses stood before him, his hand outstretched. He moved his head from side to side trying to look around the inside of the foyer, Stanley's large frame was inhibiting his view.

"Can I help you?" Stanley asked.

"You may be able to. My name is Tom Wilson

and as you can see from my truck, I'm from a local dessert shop." He dropped his hand when he realized the man before him wasn't going to shake it.

"I've never heard of this dessert shop. The only shop I know of is Baker's Dozen over on Kinsey Street." Stanley peered at him through squinty eyes.

"Yes, well, um I was wondering if perhaps. . ." Just then Roy ran down the stairs and jumped in front of his Dad.

"Hey, Mr. Wilson!" He said as Stanley laid a hand on his shoulder.

"You know this man? His Dad asked.

"Yeah, this is the Pumpkin Pie man."

Through his sunglasses, Tim Wilson's eyes widened and a smile formed on his face, small, yellow-stained teeth filling his mouth. Stanley got a whiff of his breath which reeked of stale tobacco.

"Roy, my boy!" a hand tussled the child's hair. Stanley pulled his son back away from the door.

"State your business, Mr. Wilson. Roy, why don't you run upstairs for now?" Stanley kept his eyes on the man before him.

"I'll cut to the chase, Mr. Childers, my stock of delicious pies are in desperate need of a home and I've been all over the place to no avail. Would your wife want to buy a couple? I have pumpkin, apple, and cherry. I also ha–" Stanley stopped him mid-sentence.

"Listen, my wife does all of our baking and cooking. She's worked painstakingly for the past few days for our Thanksgiving meal so I think we'll decline. I'm sorry. Have a good holiday." Stanley started to close the door.

"That's what Samantha Jenkins said to me but after some coaxing, she bought one." He shrugged his shoulders and giggled. "I heard about what happened to them. Such a shame." Stanley felt a huge knot form in his belly. The Pumpkin Pie man continued, " It would be a shame if I went back to the bakery and I still had all these pies. You sure you don't want one or two?"

"Like I said, no thank you." Stanley still felt uneasy as he shut the door in Tim Wilson's face. He looked out of the window and watched as the man got into his truck. Right before he pressed the accelerator, he stole a glance at an upstairs window of the house and saw Roy looking through it. The Pumpkin Pie man lowered his sunglasses revealing dead, cloudy eyes. Roy backed away from the glass, stunned, and realized there was a puddle of piss on the floor.

***

Wednesday, November 22nd: 11:44 p.m.

A fierce wind blew outside Roy's window as he slept. As the moon took on shadow and light, a faint whisper could be heard outside.

Roy... Roy...

He tossed and turned while his eyes were closed, the orbs within his head shifting from side to side underneath his lids. The window crept open. A mist, slow and steady filled his room until it hovered over him. Suddenly a bodily presence formed at the foot of his bed. It was tall and thin and its head tilted to one side. As the moonlight brought natural illumination into Roy's bedroom, the entity's face could be seen. It had a long nose and a slimy, slithering tongue that jutted in and out as if it was probing the air. Its eyes were wide and white with no pupils and it smiled a horrid grin full of fangs. It easily caressed the floor as it floated toward the head of the bed and as Roy laid on his back, his eyes closed tightly, facing the ceiling, the being came close to him and took a deep breath, its long skeletal fingers ever so slightly caressing the boy's cheeks. It began to speak in a low gravelly voice.

"Within my house is the sickening sweet smell of nutmeg and spice. Upon a grave, you'll dance as soon as you've eaten a slice. Scream and run as fast as you can. There is no escaping The Pumpkin Pie Man. Take another and eat your fill. It's wormy and cold and your blood will spill."

Roy, suddenly, opened his eyes to the blackness before him. His window was closed tightly and although he could feel the gooseflesh on his body, he was sweating and his pajama top held tightly to his chest. He took it off and fell back onto his pillow. As Roy drifted back to sleep, he began to dream about his family surrounding a dinner table tied to their chairs as the Pumpkin Pie man force-fed each one a piece of pie covered in maggots.

***

Thursday, November 23rd: Thanksgiving Day. 1:00

p.m.

"Roy, please help your grandmother set the table." Marjorie Childers reached into the oven and pulled out a golden brown and delicious turkey that had been slowly roasting all night long. She'd gotten up every so often in the middle of the night and basted it to perfection. Along with the turkey, there were homemade yeast rolls slathered in butter, corn on the cob, dressing, mashed potatoes, and cranberry sauce, of course–Josephine had insisted on it–and candied yams. It was the typical Thanksgiving meal complete with pumpkin pie for dessert.

After everything was settled and the family sat down in their respective chairs, Stanley began to carve the turkey, its juices flowing after every slice of the knife. They did have a lot to be thankful for despite the recent tragedy in the neighborhood. Marjorie across from Stanley and looked through the kitchen window above the sink. She noticed a man walking up their front steps.

"Someone's coming to the door," Marjorie said as she started to get up from the table.

"He's here!" Roy exclaimed as he ran to the door and opened it. Tom Wilson stood in the doorway with a square box in his hands. Stanley could feel his skin crawling off his body.

"What's he doing here?"

"I invited him!"

"Without permission." Stanley shook his head and got up from the table.

"I told you we didn't want any of your pies." He was stern with The Pumpkin Pie man, a small vein popping out on his forehead. He could feel his blood pressure rising.

"I'm sorry about this. I thought the boy had asked you if it was okay. I do have a complimentary pie though, free of charge! I need to get rid of them." His eyes appeared to be bloodshot and he rocked on his heels waiting for an answer.

"Please Dad, please," Roy begged. Stanley didn't want to disappoint his son. He looked over at Marjorie. She nodded up and down, reluctantly.

"Please come in," Stanley said. "We'll set a place for you."

***

After the meal, Tom Wilson offered to serve the family a piece of the pie he'd brought as a gift. Although Stanley had protested, he could tell Roy was eager to try it. After all, the way Tom had built up the suspense, he knew one piece wouldn't hurt anybody, and if it would get him quickly out of the house, the better.

"Whipped cream?" Tom asked. He surveyed each face that sat around the table and breathed a sigh of relief. He walked around the table and dispensed a dollop on each plate.

"You know, I always have a hard time selling these things. I'm awfully glad you all decided to try it. It's all thanks to your sweet little boy here." He stared at Roy as the boy began shoveling the orange goo into his mouth. The rest of the family followed suit. The pie was devoured in a frenzy and as Josephine took her last bite she noticed the Pumpkin Pie man grinning from ear to ear, a low, horrendous laugh beginning to come up from his throat. Soon he was laughing hysterically as one by one, the family started to convulse. He got up from the table and danced around, his clothing falling from his skeletal body. He hunched over and jumped on the table, scuttling like a cockroach. Frothy blood seeped from Marjorie's lips and she lurched forward, face falling into her empty plate with a thud. Josephine fell backward against her chair, her eyes bleeding. The last thing she saw was The Pumpkin Pie man looking down on her as she stared at the ceiling with dead eyes.

"This is so much fun!" The thing that was Tom Wilson said. "I love playing this game every single Thanksgiving! I had a hell of a time at the Jenkins' place. You should've seen them writhe and clutch their throats! They didn't have pumpkin though, they wanted the apple! I stuck razor blades inside that pie!"

Stanley fell from his chair onto the floor and slowly began to crawl to the front door. Suddenly the creature was upon him, drool falling from his mouth full of fangs.

"Oh no you don't!" the thing hissed. He pulled Stanley's head up by the hair, its sharp fingernails digging into his scalp. It began to bleed. "The game's not over, yet. Look!" The monster screamed, its voice sent a chill up Stanley's spine. He stared helplessly at Roy, hot tears streaming down his face. The creature gurgled in his ear. . .

You smell the nutmeg?. . . the cloying stench of something sugary and sweet?

Suddenly a long skeletal finger sliced through Stanley's neck, his eyes rolling back into his head. The entity released him and his head hit the floor with a bang. Stanley lay there in a crimson pool, his heart steadily pumping blood out of the wound until it stopped. The Pumpkin Pie man scurried along the floor and nestled beside Roy who was slumped over in his chair. It lifted the boy's face with gray bony hands, its white eyes wide and piercing. It whispered...

You're mine now, boy. Just like all the others. I would've taken the Jenkins' girl but the blue people came too quickly. But I have you! We have much to do to get ready for next year. A different town, maybe a city perhaps? Who knows...

Tom Wilson adjusted his bow tie straightened his milkman jacket and headed for the front door. Roy Childers laid in his arms, his head and feet dangling. The Pumpkin Pie man opened the back doors to his panel truck and threw the child into it, the body jostling against a pile of small human bones. He slammed the doors shut, fingered around his shirt pocket, and pulled out a cigar. He climbed into the driver's seat and turned the ignition. He lit the cigar, slammed the gear shift into "D" and drove down Cherry Street, just as the sun began to set.

ALLISHA MCADOO

The End

About the author: Jason Jones is an Industrial Painter by trade. He has been published in Horrorscope: A Zodiac Anthology volumes, 2 and 3 by January Ember Press, The Dark Village Anthology by Dark Village Publications, Sirens Call Publications, and the Upcoming Doors of Darkness Anthology by Terrorcore Publishing. He currently lives in Central Indiana with his wife, 2 cats, and a dog. Instagram is thehorrornovelnut76

The Importance Of Tradition

By Christopher Besonen

Father sliced the meat from the bones without breaking his gaze with me. He carved with precision as he stared into my eyes.

"You know that tradition is everything in this family. Now that you've reached adulthood, it is your turn to split the wishbone with me. But it is of extreme importance that the break be even. Do you understand?"

I nodded that I did.

"I'll nod three times, and then we each pull in our direction. When it hears the snap, it will come.

Remember, two same-sized pieces. Ready?"

I nodded that I was.

We both jerked the wishbone in opposing directions, then Father let out a shriek.

"What have you done? Your half is much larger than mine! This cannot be. Our bloodline has always managed to end up with matching halves. For centuries, the tradition was not broken."

There was a thud at the front door, then three knocks.

"We must present two even pieces," Father whimpered, sticking the smaller of the bone shards into his pocket.

Three knocks came again, harder the second time.

My wide eyes locked with my father's.

"What's out there?"

"I don't know! Nobody has ever won or lost before!"

"What do we do?"

"Go to the door. Take two of the pieces from last year, then present them as our offering."

I felt nothing but terror. I dreaded knowing what was out there, and even more dread conjured itself about lying to whatever it was.

I couldn't move. I was too scared.

Three more knocks came again. This time they were spaced out a little further which made me feel tense at the rising frustration on the opposite side of the doorframe.

Father curled up, one of his hands fumbling in his pocket with the losing shard of bone.

I started towards the door, but the loose deck board creaked, meaning whatever was knocking had stepped off of our porch.

Then father screamed as if he were being murdered. He grabbed me by my shoulders and shook me.

"You broke another tradition by not answering the

door! Oh, what have you done?"

Father sobbed.

I studied the natural etches of the woodwork, my mind blank. I could feel the rate of my heart pulsing in my wrists.

It took Father a week to break his state of paranoia. By the end of December, things were back to normal, if you subtract his reoccurring nightmares of him being flayed alive.

On the first of January, Father woke me up by his frantic yelling and cursing. I rushed to his room, then I saw the root cause of his manic episode. The entire floor was covered in whittled branches with asymmetrical sides.

"They're makeshift wishbones," Father laughed, his brain cracking along with his vocal tone.

He let out a nervous giggle every time one of them snapped as we picked them up.

It was summer when Father finally left his sanity behind him. He would never be the same after three knocks on his window brought him out of a deep sleep. Metal points scraped along the glass.

"It's coming! We destroyed our Thanksgiving covenant, and it demands retribution!"

Father would repeat those exact words nightly, all through the months when the leaves were changing. His night terrors were elevated by now.

"It sometimes comes to see me in my dreams. It speaks to me and condemns us for our offenses. It only casts itself as a shadow. Tonight, it told me about the cruel death by razor wire at the hands of our ancestors. How the drops of blood upon a budding tree were responsible for it being reborn," he repeated over and over one night, standing at the foot of my bed, his pitch elevating with each repeat until I finally awoke.

Once I was awake, his tone leveled off, but the phrase continued being uttered until the following afternoon.

A year went by, and we saw financial ruin. Father was irrational and unable to work. He spent most of his days muttering about the upcoming holiday. I was fired from every job that I managed to snag. We were being foreclosed on, living out the final month of our cursed year, when three knocks tapped against the front door one night.

Father yelped.

We had broken the tradition again. This year we didn't bother with a turkey. Couldn't afford it. Instead, we had cereal with powdered milk.

"Go and see what it wants," Father begged.

I made my way to the door, then I flung it open, and a high-pitched sound of panic escaped my throat.

"I smell offense," it said with a voice I could only comprehend subconsciously.

It likely used to be human, but a tree and razor wire had overtaken his entire system. Neither the pointy wire nor the bark stayed stationary.

They kept him in agony, I would guess, as he dripped bloody wood shavings without ceasing. He reached out an arm, and then a pair of uneven phalanges caressed my cheek. As the skin on my face was pricked, my subconscious heard the voice again.

"Three offenses. First, the uneven wishbone to mock my impairments. Then you left my offering collection unanswered. Finally, you dared not make amends this year by making no attempt to celebrate or be thankful. So, three it will be, three kinds of saws to remove the layers of your father's anatomy. This will start a new tradition, one that you will pass down or meet the same fate. A victim must be sacrificed, and their skeleton offered to me on this day, it must be deboned layer by layer. Carve and peel, that's the method I like. You'll find yours."

Father was then grabbed by tentacles of razor points and was taken to have his layers removed by three types of saws.

"Generations of our bloodline's pact and you're the only one to ever fail! My murder is on your hands," Father called out to me.

I smiled, feeling grateful to live as Father squealed

for mercy.

My family was always faithful to custom, and I was thankful to birth a new tradition.

The End

About the author :

Christopher Besonen can usually be found in either Missouri or Ohio depending on the year. He is the author of 10 books that create a Puzzle Series. The more you read, the more pieces connect. All titles can also work as standalone.

Linktr.ee/BesonenHorror

Besonen is on most social platforms: #BesonenHorror

Find out Besonen's opinion on the Indie Horror books he is reading at UncomfortablyDark.com/besonenbreakdowns Also by:

"Network": a technological, imaginative Horror novella.

https://books2read.com/u/b5X7Aw

https://godless.com/collections/christopher-besonen/products/network-by-christopher-besonen

Barnyard Blood

By Ivan K. Conway

"Stanford Hawthorne, you're a good man but a terrible liar!" Elenore snapped at her husband.

"I swear, I burned it!" he vowed while backing into their kitchen counter.

"We tried that years ago!" was her outraged

reminder.

He wanly smiled after scratching his beard. "We didn't sprinkle holy water on its ashes last time."

Recalling that past attempt made Elenore quiver. Their fireplace had seemingly burned the bone grimoire to cinders. Yet, it regrew seconds later inside some sort of embryonic sac.

"You expect me to believe it was that easy?! *The Book of Everlasting Love* is older than this country!" she protested before stomping their farmhouse floorboards.

It was true. This particular copy had supposedly been smuggled into the colonies by heretical Pilgrims.

"If it could be destroyed by any pastor with a baptismal and a firepit, it wouldn't be here!" concluded Elenore.

His wrinkled brow furrowed before he ran a calloused hand through his white locks. Elenore knew she'd won.

So did he. That didn't stop him, however. "That book is evil, Elenore. I know you know that."

Even if she hadn't spent years hanging witches, she would've known. Nothing good came of grimoires made from human body parts.

Tears burned trails down her weather-beaten cheeks. "I don't care anymore, Stan. I don't wanna be righteous. I just want my grandbaby back."

"Dark magic takes more than it gives," he warned even as he grew teary. "We'd all regret using it. Emily most of all."

Elenore wiped her eyes on the sleeve of her red blouse. "You don't know that! She didn't want the plague to take her, Stan! She died scared and crying!"

He handed her the blue handkerchief he stored in his overalls pocket. "She's in a better place now, sweetheart. She's with Jack and Gloria now. Where she belongs."

"To Hell with that and to Hell with you!" bawled Elenore before grabbing a shovel beside the screen door. "I'll go find it myself!"

***

Elenore dashed into the autumn afternoon. The wind was swaying her gray bangs and porch swing. It also sent shivers through the empty prairie beyond.

Stan shoved open the front door behind her. "Elenore, please!"

Her grip on that shovel tightened. She then made a beeline for the shed. "Stay outta my way!"

She'd found it last week. It'd sprouted where Stan slaughtered hogs for holiday ham.

"Thought you were clever, didn't ya?" she observed while storming into the green shack. "You *knew* I never had the stomach for killing animals and never liked the place. Course, *I knew you knew!* That's why it's the first place I checked!"

And there it stood. Growing out of the bloodstained dirt floor was a white sapling as tall as Elenore's knee.

Stan's stunned horror was audible as he

arrived beside her. "My God…"

"God had nothing to do with this," Elenore remarked with shared disgust.

The tree's unnatural nature was obvious. Its trunk and branches were white bone, and its leaves were throbbing skin.

After a hard swallow, Elenore started digging up the wretched thing.

"Leave it alone, Elenore. Leave it alone," her husband pled.

It was too late. She now held the sapling by its stem. As she guessed, *The Book of Everlasting Love* hung from its roots like a grotesque bulb.

"Pa told me about things like this," she recounted with a shudder. "Said trees of bone sometimes grew where witches were buried. Never knew of any growing from their grimoires though."

Her greasy find felt both cold and hot at once. It also stank of incense, roses, and rot.

She tried freeing the book from its roots to

no avail. "Blast it! Gonna need a knife! Stan-"

Suddenly, that sapling disintegrated and its freed tome fell into the dirt.

***

Elenore's head sank onto their kitchen table. She then slammed that table with her fist. "God dammit, Stan!"

Sitting beside her was that open grimoire. Every page of human skin had been washed clean with holy water.

"We couldn't destroy it. And it was too dangerous to let fall into evil hands," explained Stan apologetically. He consolingly gripped her shoulder. "So, I improvised. Still surprised it even worked."

She couldn't completely blame him. They'd been neutralizing such wicked relics for years. Nobody could've foreseen her wanting to use one herself.

"This ain't over yet," growled Elenore as she lifted her head. "My pa didn't raise no quitter!"

Pig's blood had made a hellish tree grow from the tome. This made Elenore wonder what human blood might do.

She sat up and grabbed a steak knife beside the book.

"Honey," Stan said with alarm, "What are you-"

That knife made a wet whistle when Elenore slid it across her palm. She then squeezed her bleeding fist over the grimoire. Its bone cover soaked up her gore but did nothing else.

Stan's shoulders dipped in relief. He still did his best to be sympathetic, however. "Well, it was an interesting idea."

"Not yet!" Elenore desperately opened the book to its first skin pages. "Not yet!"

Elenore's spilled blood hit those macabre sheets with soft splats. Her vital fluid then began to twist and spread across them.

"Look! Look, love! It's working!" exclaimed Elenore with jubilant sobs. "It's working!"

When they'd first pried the book from a warlock's bullet-ridden corpse, its words were Latin. Yet, the new text forming from Elenore's blood was English.

"Amazing," she uttered with awe, "It's as if it *wants* to be understood. As if it *wants* to be read."

Stan moved to grab the grimoire. "Honey, this has to stop."

"No!" shrieked Elenore snatching her tome from the table. She then rushed up their staircase to the bedroom. "This can't stop! Not now! Not ever!"

***

The ritual was about ten pages long. Elenore's gore ceased to spread through her book once its instructions were fully written. Yet, its promised power was exactly what she needed.

"Elenore! Elenore!" begged Stan while knocking on their locked bedroom door. "Please! Let me in!"

She'd just finished wrapping her cut hand

in Stan's bandanna. This completed, she gave a resigned sigh. "Fine. But I'm locking you out again if I even see *a drop* of holy water."

Stan entered cautiously once she unlocked the door. He looked both relieved and exasperated. "Honey, are you alright?"

"A bit woozy from blood loss," she admitted brushing her forehead. "But I'll live."

"And the book?" he leerily added.

Elenore couldn't help feeling strange pride as she opened her grimoire. "This is it, Stan. Just what I wanted. It's as if *The Book of Everlasting Love* knew."

He carefully took her tome and began reading it. His face grew paler with each turned page. "Elenore, do you realize what this ritual will do?"

"It'll bring our grandbaby back," excitedly replied a trembling Elenore. "And just in time for Thanksgiving, too! Just think! We'll be able to have Thanksgiving dinner as a family again!"

"This ritual would bring Emily back as *a vampire*, Elenore! You'd be condemning our granddaughter to an eternity as a bloodsucking monster!"

"She'd never get sick, Stan! She'd never die!" retorted Elenore tearfully snatching back her book.

Stan's eyes also grew teary as his head shook. "Exactly! She'd never get to grow up! She'd never stop craving blood! She'd never be reunited with her parents in Heaven!"

Elenore clutched her tome under one arm and grabbed her shovel with the other. "We've got enough gold stashed away to support her forever! And we've got plenty of livestock! What difference would it make feeding her animal blood instead of meat?! And we've raised her a lot longer than Jack and Gloria ever have!"

"Elenore, I love you," declared Stan blocking off their bedroom doorway. "I always have and I always will. But I'm *never* letting you do this!"

Her head dipped before she smiled faintly. "I

know. I love you, too. Forever and for always. And I figured you'd do something like this."

Stan's right brow rose curiously.

"Which is why I prepared for it," she announced before tugging aside their bedroom curtains.

His eyes widened upon seeing the exposed bedsheet rope she'd nailed to their windowsill.

Before he could make another move, Elenore started shimmying down her improvised climbing tool. "See ya at our granddaughter's grave!"

***

Elenore watched from their kitchen window as Stan guarded Emily's tombstone. He thought he'd beaten her there. But she'd exhumed Emily's remains a week ago.

"Sorry for tricking you, darlin'," Elenore admitted with a wince. She then uncapped a large barrel beside her. "Reckon that's my first fib to you since we started courting. But when all's said and done, you'll understand. I swear."

Inside the cask was Emily's body buried in salt. Aside from her white dress and black hair, the mummified corpse was unrecognizable.

"Wonder how long it'll take him to figure it out," Elenore pondered as she gently placed Emily on the floor. "Man's always had more book smarts than good sense."

They'd first met when Stan became St. Crow's new head priest. The church had supplied her with witch-hunting equipment for years. But it'd never had a more handsome holy roller.

"Know your great-grandpappy wasn't too fond of him," she wistfully related to Emily while preparing the ritual. "Said the boy was too soft. Too pompous. More fit to be a librarian than a soldier of God."

Pa had been wrong though. A particularly nasty coven killed him one night and chased Elenore to the church. They would've murdered her, too, had Stan not helped her kill them first.

"We've been inseparable ever since,"

recounted Elenore with a sad smile. "Was quite a scandal when he left the priesthood for me. Folks in our hometown still call me a harlot for that. But I reckon we did more good together than he ever would've done behind a pulpit."

They'd hunted all sorts of supernatural evils over the years. Witches especially. Only after Elenore's first pregnancy did they finally retire to their farmhouse outside of Dry Rose.

She paused to admire her work. "Think it's ready."

In accordance with the book's instructions, salt was laid in a dove skull shape. Animal bones encircled it, and blood runes lined the circle's outer edges.

"Almost forgot!" exclaimed Elenore snapping her fingers. "Still need native soil!"

Elenore emptied several flowerpots worth of dirt into the bone circle. This complete, she then laid Emily on top of that salt sigil.

The locked screen door began rattling from Stan's desperate attempts to open it. "Elenore!

Don't do this! Elenore!"

"You'll see, darlin'. When we're all eating Thanksgiving dinner together, you'll see," swore Elenore through guilty tears.

As she lifted her hand over the ceremonial circle, she intoned the ritual's incantation. Its words chilled her veins and stung her tongue.

"Emily will outlive us, too, Elenore! We won't ever see her in Heaven! Elenore! Elenore!" Stan wailed.

And still, she repeated the chant. "By the blood. By the soil. By the salt of the sea. Ildelfel, Lord of the Dead, return my love to me. By the air. By the stone. By the flesh and the bone. Ildelfel, Lord of Love, call my beloved home. By the hope. By your word. By my breath do I plea. Ildelfel, Keeper of my Soul, unite us for eternity!"

After her third recitation, Elenore's magical seal became bright light and snowy feathers filled the air.

"No!" was Stan's devastated howl.

That ceremonial circle soon vanished with the feathers. Emily remained, however. Her body had turned as pale as her tattered dress. And the child's raven hair trailed to her feet. She otherwise appeared pristine.

"Emily?" whispered a hopeful Elenore.

Emily's eyes snapped open to reveal they'd become opaque white orbs. She then gave Elenore a fang-filled smile. "Granny, I missed you."

***

Shielded from the sun by Elenore's black umbrella, Emily accompanied her outside.

Elenore was weeping happily with their every step. The little hand she held was clawed and cold. But it was her grandbaby's.

Meanwhile, Stan was sobbing on their porch swing. Elenore doubted he wept for the same reason she did. But she hoped to change that.

"Stan. Stan, honey, look," encouraged Elenore as her husband came into view. "Our angel's back!"

Stan's body stiffened. He then slowly turned to face his undead granddaughter.

"Grampa!" cheered an elated Emily as their eyes met.

He just gave her a haunted stare.

Slowly, that newly risen vampire approached him with open arms. "Grampa, I missed you!"

"No," Stan tearfully muttered as he scooted sideways. "No. Keep that thing away from me! That thing is not our grandchild!"

This didn't deter Emily. She instead wrapped him in a tight hug. "Grampa!"

Stan didn't return the embrace. He just sat there frozen. His left eye started twitching.

Those two stayed that way for nearly a minute. It brought a hint of doubt into Elenore's head. She began biting her lip with worry.

But, finally, something broke in her husband. He let out a loud sob before snatching their granddaughter tightly. "Oh, Emily! God help us!

Emily!"

***

Emily now slept in a casket on her bed. And she was daily fed blood from their family's slaughtered livestock. Otherwise, the week leading to Thanksgiving felt remarkably normal.

Elenore couldn't help delightedly laughing as she assessed her latest experiment with the grimoire. "This is perfect! Here's a ritual that'll keep blood from spoiling! Who knew that's the effect turkey gore would have?!"

So far, she'd exposed her tome to the vital fluids of several animals. Each kind of blood filled the book with more writing. This made her anxious to test new human samples.

Stan was frowning at her from across the kitchen table. "Elenore, I thought we agreed to rebury that vile thing."

She gave a dismissive wave. "Oh, stop worrying! We will! But look at this! This ritual will help us store extra blood for Emily! Isn't it wonderful?!"

Her husband's frown only deepened. "Elenore, you haven't forgotten how evil that tome is, have you? I mean, just look at it."

This earned her halfhearted shrug. "I don't know, darlin'. Lately, it's struck me as kinda pretty. In a macabre sorta way."

Images of dried flowers, skeletal birds, and filigree patterns were carved into its bone cover. And a dove skull loomed prominently over the Latin title. Surprised her that she'd never appreciated this artistry before.

Stan took a hesitant breath before speaking again. "You do remember that we believe in hanging witches and not emulating them?"

His question made her flinch as if struck. "Of course, I do! What I'm doing is completely different!"

Her husband said nothing. But concern and skepticism twisted his face.

That sight gave her brief doubts. But Elenore quickly brushed them off. "Witches use magic for evil ends. And we haven't done that! Have we? I mean, we brought Emily back! You don't regret it, right?"

He ran a hand through his hair again. Stan then glanced uncomfortably at the ceiling. Their grandbaby was sleeping soundly upstairs. "I... suppose. But please, be careful, honey."

Elenore glanced between him and the bloodstained steak knife by the grimoire. "You know, your blood might affect the book, too. Maybe-"

Stan's response was to stand up. "I better get tonight's dinner ready for Emily. I'll see you later."

"Alright," said Elenore as her shoulders sank in disappointment. She then gave him a conciliatory grin. "Happy Thanksgiving, by the way."

This made him pause at the door before turning to her and smiling back. "Thank you. Happy Thanksgiving, honey."

Elenore felt her cheeks redden as he left for the barn. Even after all these years, Stan still made her heart flutter.

***

Emily was helping set the dinner table. Her eyes grew wide as she regarded four bowls laid in front of her chair. "Granny, are all these for me?"

Elenore gave her a wary smile while preparing their turkey on the kitchen counter. "That's right, sweetheart. Each bowl will have the blood of a different animal."

Honestly, Elenore didn't think the blood's source impacted its flavor. But she didn't want Emily's Thanksgiving feast to be too boring.

Emily's fanged grin glittered in the candlelight. "Yay! I wish every day was Thanksgiving!"

It was hard for Elenore not to cringe. She knew Emily yearned for more vital fluid than they were providing her.

"It is a fun day, isn't it? Now, go wash up," urged Elenore with forced cheer.

"Okay," said the vampire rushing upstairs. Her red dress fluttered and her ponytail bobbed with every excited footfall.

Stan then entered the farmhouse with two iron buckets in tow. He looked tired and sweaty.

She gave him a weak grin. "Thank ya, darlin'."

He sighed upon leaving those buckets at her feet. "That's our last cow and chicken."

"We'll use the meat," she reassured him. "You know we will."

"Emily asks for more blood every day," was Stan's leery response.

Elenore frowned. "Well, just go down to Dry Rose and get us another cow and some more chickens."

Fresh worry filled Stan's face. "Will you be safe while I'm gone?"

This earned Elenore's stunned gape. "What are you suggesting?"

Her husband shuddered. "I've caught Emily watching us while we sleep."

Elenore's head shook. "You must've been dreaming."

"Elenore," Stan pressed before wiping his brow. "How long do you think she'll stay sated on the blood of chickens, cows, and goats?"

"Emily loves us!" snapped back Elenore. "And she wouldn't hurt a fly! She's our sweet angel!"

"Granny!" chipperly yelled their granddaughter skipping down the stairs. "I'm all done!"

Hurriedly, Elenore flashed her spouse a warning look before smiling at Emily. "Wonderful, hun! Then as soon as your grandpa gets washed up, we can get this Thanksgiving dinner started!"

"Yay! I'm starving!" cheered Emily with a ravenous grin.

***

"Hmm hmm!" said Emily setting down her last emptied bowl. "So good! Thank you, Granny and Grampa!"

Their table's stink of gore made Elenore nauseous. She could tell her husband felt similarly. Yet, they'd forced down bites of turkey and mashed potatoes for Emily's sake.

Emily's corpselike eyes keenly studied her grandparents. "So, what's for dessert?"

Stan gave a start and Elenore's jaw dropped. They then traded glances before Elenore hesitantly answered, "I'm sorry, sweetheart. But that's all the animal blood we have right now."

"But I'm still hungry!" the crestfallen vampire whined.

Loud knocks at the door made everyone jump.

"Good heavens!" Elenore exclaimed with widening eyes. "It's Jeremiah!"

She and Stan had invited their pastor for Thanksgiving last month. Elenore had completely forgotten.

"What do we do?! God only knows how he'd react if he sees Emily!" was Stan's panicked observation.

Emily regarded this crisis with calm curiosity.

Meanwhile, Elenore glanced guiltily at their kitchen window. "I've got an idea. Cough loudly when I open the door. I'll try to handle the rest."

He knowingly nodded as the pastor's knocks resumed.

She then cracked the door open and Stan coughed on cue. Elenore followed this by giving their forgotten guest an apologetic smile. "Jeremiah! Happy Thanksgiving! So good to see you!"

The round man brushed his green coat and trousers before tipping his matching bowler hat. "Happy Thanksgiving, you two! Sorry, I'm late! The roads were awful! Hope you don't mind that I left the horses in your barn!"

His black carriage was visible in front of the house. Elenore inwardly groaned knowing how much time it'd take to re-hitching those steeds to the vehicle.

Emily sat up and started sniffing. "Something smells tasty!"

Stan gave a scolding hush.

Jeremiah crinkled his brow and stroked his cinnamon beard. "Now, that's a familiar voice! Where've I heard it before?"

Was all Elenore could do not to facepalm. Jeremiah had known Emily from baptism to the funeral. Of course, he'd recognize her voice! She should've quieted the vampire in advance.

"My third cousins stopped by for a visit," Elenore quickly lied. "Unfortunately, she's brought a nasty cold with her. Poor Stan's already caught it. We'd hate for you to get it, too."

On cue, Stan started coughing again.

Elenore glanced back at the kitchen before biting her lip. "Tell ya what, Jeremiah, how about I send you home with some leftovers? That way, you can avoid getting sick while still getting to enjoy our home cooking."

The pastor dismissively waved his meaty

hand. "Bah! Nonsense! I've got an ironclad constitution and our Lord's protection! And nothing better flavors food than a good company!"

Whiffs of Emily's gory feast still hung in the air. Elenore desperately hoped Jeremiah didn't notice. "Believe me, we wouldn't be good company tonight. Most of us are sick and crabby right now. But thank you for offering."

To Elenore's relief, Jeremiah's wide head sank in defeat. "Fair enough. I'll be sure to pray y'all get better soon."

Stan discreetly slipped her a plate of food from behind the door. She was grateful enough to kiss him. Instead, she handed the meal to their pastor. "Here ya go, Jeremiah. Happy Thanksgiving!"

This seemed to brighten Jeremiah's mood. He grinned upon taking the leftovers. "Happy Thanksgiving to you all! Goodbye and God bless!"

"Goodbye, Pastor Jeremiah!" added a cheerful Emily.

Recognition filled Jeremiah's face as it went

whiter than milk. "It can't be..."

Their pastor shoved past them and stumbled into the kitchen. He dropped his plate at the sight of Emily.

"Hi!" greeted that seated vampire while waving at him. "You smell good!"

"What is this?!" Jeremiah yelled in baffled horror. "Emily's dead! I presided over her funeral! What is this?!"

Emily giggled before pointing to *The Book of Everlasting Love* on their counter. "Granny brought me back with that magic book! Didn't ya, Granny?!"

Jeremiah's fat forefinger then pointed condemningly at Elenore. "Witch! My God, I don't believe it! You're a witch!"

The accusation left Elenore gaping in shock.

"The town's hearing about this!" the priest declared. "This is an abomination! You and that unholy imp you've summoned!"

Stan grasped Jeremiah's shoulders.

"Jeremiah, please calm down!"

"Don't tell me to calm down!" snapped the holy roller fighting to shake Stan loose. His efforts made the two men fall in a heap.

"Stanford! Are you alright?!" Elenore asked rushing to untangle the pair.

Jeremiah's head lifted to reveal a trail of blood flowing down his nose. "You stay away, you wicked warlock!"

Emily's sniffing intensified. "Is that human blood? It smells yummy!"

"Honey, stay back!" shouted Elenore to her grandchild. But Emily was gone.

Stan gave a start. "Oh, God!"

Elenore's gaze followed her husband's upward. Emily was skittering across the ceiling like a caffeinated spider. And she was heading straight for their dinner guest.

Jeremiah saw the oncoming vampire, too, and scrambled to his feet. He then reached under his coat.

Emily was faster. She pounced on the pastor and pinned him to the floor.

"Emily, no!" Stan yelled in terror.

That vampire was deaf to the world as her petite body got bathed in Jeremiah's gore. Emily's eyes were glowing and her jaws had opened to an inhuman width. Elenore barely recognized her.

Then Emily let out a piercing shriek and fled her prey as he presented a silver cross. He yelled zealously even as blood continued pumping out his bitten throat. "Back! Back, you demon!"

"It hurts! Grannie! Grampa! It hurts! Make him stop!" tearfully wailed Emily as she curled into a ball under the table.

Elenore unthinkingly rushed to shield her grandbaby. "Jeremiah, that's enough!"

"I'm not hearing another word out of you, demon worshipper!" was Jeremiah's retort as he stood back up and limped towards the door. "I'll be back tomorrow! And I'm bringing a lynch mob with-"

His threat was cut off by Stan beaning him with a frying pan. That pastor then began twitching as he lay prone and bleeding on the floor.

"Emily? Elenore? Are you two alright?" asked Stan between hard breaths.

Elenore nodded before slipping Jeremiah's cross into her skirt pocket.

In the meantime, Emily had resumed sucking on Jeremiah's neck wounds.

"What've I done?!" asked a horrified Elenore at the carnage in front of her.

"All *we've* done," Stan answered while setting that bloodstained frying pan on the counter, "Is love our granddaughter."

At last, Emily finished feeding. The thing that was once their sweet angel licked her gore-smeared face and yawned. "That was *so* good! Can I go to bed now?"

Elenore hesitantly nodded. "Of course, sweetheart. Go wash up and we can read you a bedtime story."

Their granddaughter nodded with a sleepy smile before heading upstairs. She would've appeared normal if not covered in vital fluid. "Okay. Happy Thanksgiving, Grannie, and Grampa! Love you!"

"Happy Thanksgiving, sweetheart. We love you, too," Elenore replied before shuddering and grasping Jeremiah's cross tight.

Upon Emily's departure, Stan turned to *The Book of Everlasting Love*. "Looks like there's still some of Jeremiah's blood left if you-"

Elenore's head shook. "Think I'm done fiddling with that damn time."

He absently nodded. "We'd best burn Jeremiah before he turns into a vampire, too. I'll go to Goldcross tomorrow and trade his horses and wagon. That ought to be far away enough that no one will recognize them."

"Folks in town will still wonder where he's gone," she fretted.

He comfortingly clasped her shoulders. "It's a long way between here and Dry Rose. And the roads today were awful. *Anything* could've happened to him."

"Right. *Anything*," she concurred conspiratorially before kissing his hand. "Stan, I love you."

Stan kissed her head. "I love you, too, honey. And, for whatever it's worth, Happy Thanksgiving."

A nervous laugh escaped her lips. "Happy Thanksgiving, darlin'. And Stan?"

"Hmm?" he replied with a curious look.

"Please be sure to buy us some chickens in Goldcross tomorrow," said Elenore glancing fearfully up at their ceiling.

Stan hugged her tight. "Will do. Remember, there's a barrel of holy water in the barn. And I think we still have some silver bullets saved in the closet. Just in case you ever need them."

They could hear Emily giggle in her room. The once wonderful sound made Elenore shiver.

The end

About the author: Ivan K. Conway wrote his first book at four years old using crayons and construction paper. He's rarely stopped writing since. Yet, it was only after graduating from Carroll College that he decided to share his stories with the world. His debut short story, "Til Death", can be found in the Cursed Items Anthology. His debut novel, Goblins & Gunslingers: Bad Blood, is available on Amazon. Find him on Facebook, Goodreads, and Instagram.

Thanksgiving at the Coopers' House
By Wade Cox

Devin knelt in front of his 6-year-old son. "Listen, Jake, you're growing up awful fast. And I think it's time you started taking on more responsibilities. How would you like to go out with me to get Thanksgiving dinner?"

"Can I, Dad? I've always wanted to help you and Mom out!"

"Sure thing, buddy. Get your coat, it's chilly today." The wind whipped all around their small house and threatened to rip shingles right off their roof. While Jake went to the closet to get his light blue winter coat, Devin walked into the kitchen, turning his attention to Carol. "Honey, Jake and I are going out to pick up Thanksgiving dinner. We should be back before dark."

"Be sure that you are. I'll have everything

else ready at 6. Try to be back here by 5." They kissed a quick peck as Jake ran by them putting on his jacket. "C'mon, Dad!"

"I guess I'd better go. Bye."

Devin crossed their wooden front porch and hobbled down the three steps to the driveway. He was only thirty-six, but ten years of doing roofing work had been hell on his knees. Once he and Jake were in the pickup and buckled up, they peeled off toward town.

Fifteen minutes later, they crossed the line into the corporate limits of Cockburn, WV, a spec on the map that was only held down by the railroad. Driving along the main drag, Devin talked to Jake about this and that, he asked about school and Little League. When the subject turned to girls, Jake seemed to get embarrassed. Maybe he had a little girlfriend at school, but it was like pulling teeth to get him to talk about it.

Before he got to what laughingly passed for downtown, Devin turned right at Miss Julie's Bakery and went across the railroad tracks. A mile down the road, the pavement ran out, and the road turned to dirt. "When are we gonna get there, Dad?"

"Won't be long now, Jake."

They drove for a few more miles until Devin spotted an emerald-green Subaru Outback with the hood up, pulled off to the side of the road. Beside it, a woman stood in a black summer dress with white polka dots. Steam poured out of the engine.

Devin pulled up behind her and parked the truck. Off came the seat belt, and on went the Nashville Predators baseball cap. He slowly got out and strolled up to the front of the Subaru. "You look like you're in a spot of trouble."

From the ruby-red lips came an angelic voice. "You could say that. Sad to say, I don't know the first thing about engines. I tried to call for help, but I can't get signal out here."

"Nobody can. It's the mountains. They kill everything around here. 'Fraid I don't know a lot about engines, myself, but I'd be happy to give you a lift into town. My brother-in-law Tommy owns a wrecker, and he can come out and tow you to his garage in town."

"OK. Normally I don't accept lifts from strangers, but you look like a good guy. Besides, you've got a kid with you. How bad could you be, right?"

They piled in Devin's beat-up old Chevy pickup and headed back into town. Along the way, they chatted about this and that. Devin and Jake learned that their passenger's name was Desirae. She lived up in Charleston, where she was a CPA. That day, with it being Thanksgiving, she was headed down to her parents' house in Nashville for a family Thanksgiving. GPS wouldn't even pick up out here because of the interference, so she was back to paper maps and was following the route as best as she could until it led back to the highway.

Devin just let her talk, but Jake was the first one to invite her to Thanksgiving dinner. She said that was very sweet of him, but she politely declined, and said she had her own family to get back to. Once they were back in town, Devin drove over to his brother-in-law's garage and got out of the truck. He walked around the place long enough to find Tommy with his head down in a 2012 Toyota Camry. "Tommy!" yelled Devin, causing his brother-in-law to jump, and at the same time, drop his wrench in the engine block.

Tommy slowly turned around and recognized Devin immediately. "Jesus, Devin. You scared the hell out of me."

"Sorry about that, Tommy. I have a little problem. Look out there in the parking lot. You see that real looker sittin' in my truck?"

"Yeah. Hot Damn! How'd you score a split-tail like that? She's even hotter than your wife."

Devin shuddered in disgust. "The next time I hear you talk about your sister like that, I'm going to vomit in your mouth. My name's Desirae. Her car broke down outside of town. I need you to take your wrecker out there and go pick it up and bring it back here."

Tommy wiped his hands on a red rag he'd had in his back pocket and then threw it down on the engine. "Hell, I guess I can do that. I need a break from this old beater, anyway."

When Tommy asked, Devin told him where to find the car, and Tommy went to Devin's truck to talk to Desirae. Whatever he said must have been charming enough, because she got out of the truck and climbed in the wrecker with him. Just before Tommy got in, he asked Devin to stay and look after the shop for about half an hour so he wouldn't have to put his tools away and lock up. Devin said he would.

Thirty-seven minutes later, they were back at the station, towing Desirae's emerald-green Subaru Outback. Another thirty minutes after that and not only did Tommy have the Outback down, but he'd looked under the hood and found the problem. "Listen, lady, I..."

"Desirae."

"Listen, Desirae, I hate to be the bearer of bad news, but your water pump is shot. I don't have another one in the garage that will fit your car, and with the holiday weekend, I wouldn't be able to get one before Tuesday."

"Aren't there any other garages in town?"

"You've never been here before, have you?"

"I guess that's a no."

"You guess correctly."

Devin looked at her with a drop of hope in his eye. "My offer still stands. You're welcome at

Thanksgiving dinner if you want to come. At the very least, we have a phone, and you could call your family and tell them you'll be along when you can."

After thinking about it for half a heartbeat, Desirae decided that, yes, she would accept the redneck's hospitality. Worse things have happened, she was sure of that.

"Anyway, Tommy, I guess we'll head back to the house now. Are you still coming by for Thanksgiving dinner after you close up?"

"I'm still invited, right?"

"Of course."

"Alright, then. I'll see you later."

Desirae piled into the beat-up old Chevy truck with Jake and Devin, and the gravel flew as he peeled out of the unpaved lot.

Tommy stood there wiping his hands on his rag and shaking his head. He mumbled to himself, "Damn, baby. I hate to see you go, but I love to watch you leave."

On the way home, Devin and Jake kept the conversation going, asking Desirae about her hobbies and what she did outside of work. It seemed like harmless enough chit-chat. She was the athletic type. She spent an hour in the gym three days a week, either doing cardio or weight training. On the weekends, she sometimes ran

5K races. That knowledge sailed right over Jake's head, but Devin filed it away as a very good thing.

After a short drive out of town, they arrived back at Devin's home. Carol stood at the screen door and watched them get out of the truck with their passenger. "See, honey," Devin said, as he shut the driver's side door, "told you I'd be back before five, and it's only three-fifteen now."

Almost sarcastically, Carol shot back, "Yes, you're very good. And who is this you've brought to us?"

"Good Afternoon, and Happy Thanksgiving. I'm Desirae. My car broke down just outside of town, and your husband and son were nice enough to pick me up and invite me to join you."

"Well, then. Welcome aboard. I'm Carol."

As soon as Desirae got to the porch, she could smell through the screen all the delicious trimmings of a wonderful Thanksgiving dinner. She had no sooner gotten through the door when she turned and remarked to Carol how wonderful it smelled in her kitchen.

Devin walked through the door about that time, with Jake nipping at his heels. He kissed Carol on the way in. "Desirae, I guess the first thing you want to do is use the phone. I'll give you the quick tour, and then show you where the phone is in the bedroom." He showed her through the small one-level ranch house except for the room that was closed off with no window. When she inquired as to what was in that room, he told her he'd show her later, which she found more than a little bit odd.

First, he pointed down the hall toward the bedroom on the left and told Desirae she could use the phone in there to make her call. She excused herself and disappeared down the hall to do just that, calling her mother collect.

At first, her mother was apprehensive to accept a collect call from someplace called Cockburn, WV, that she'd never heard of, but she did anyway. She was quickly glad that she did when Desirae came on the line and explained why she wasn't there for Thanksgiving dinner, and that it didn't look like she was going to be. Her mother was, of course, disappointed, but was thankful to know that she was safe at least.

With her phone call wrapped up, she rejoined the family in the kitchen. Devin said that dinner was going to be in a few hours and to pass the time, they could play cards at the kitchen table. Ever the gambler, and a frequent guest at the Greenbrier, Desirae thought she'd educate these people about card games. She took a seat at the table across from Devin while Carol resumed her place at the stove. Jake could be heard in another part of the house.

After a quick discussion, they settled on Gin Rummy. Devin dealt out 10 cards to Desirae and 10 to himself, turning up the next card. "You go first," he said.

Jake rummaged around in his room until he found his wooden Louisville Slugger bat and quietly removed it from his closet. Doing his best to be quiet, he crept down the hall toward the kitchen.

Desirae picked up the King of Diamonds, laid down three 5's, and discarded a Jack of Clubs.

Devin picked up that Jack of Clubs and then played three Jacks, discarding the 8 of Hearts.

"Nice."

"Thank you."

From behind Desirae, Jake quietly snuck up and swung the bat as hard as he could at her head, instantly knocking her head against the wall and rendering her unconscious.

"I did it, Dad! I got our Thanksgiving dinner!"

"Yes, you did, Jake. You did great. You were very patient during the hunt; you played your part perfectly. Now, go unlock my garage door for me."

While Jake disappeared to go do his father's bidding, Devin bent over and picked up the bloody lump in front of him.

"It's about time. You two played with your food long enough," Carol remarked, "Now cut the bitch up. I'm getting hungry."

It wasn't a long trip across the hall out of the kitchen and into the previously locked white door. Inside was a makeshift butchering station. Two sawhorses topped by a door served as a table. He laid her on the table and tied her down with a 25-ft extension cord. She stirred and moaned as he did, and when she slowly shook her head, the pool of blood leaking from its back was visible. Moaning signaled that she was waking up.

"What the hell? Where am I?" Desirae struggled and squirmed, but it was useless under the extension cord that fixed her to the table.

"Remember that room I promised to show you? Welcome to my slaughterhouse."

With all the air she could muster, Desirae started to let out a blood-curdling scream. "HELP!"

Halfway through the word, Devin slapped a piece of silver duct tape over her mouth, immediately stifling the scream. To add insult to injury, he planted a long slow kiss on top of the duct tape.

"Damn, baby. You sure are fine, and I wish things were different, but they're not, and that's that. I'm glad you told me about all that exercising you did because it means there's less fat on you. Better meat." He grabbed a pair of scissors and started at the bottom, cutting off her sun dress. When he had cut off the dress, and Desirae lay there helpless in her bra and panties, Devin thought he had stolen a moment of fleeting pleasure. He ran his hand up the length of her thigh to her crotch and squeezed, then to her breasts and squeezed again.

Just then, the door to the kitchen opened. "Devin! I'd better not catch you playing with your food again, just butcher the bitch. I catch you having sex with another one, and you'll be the one on the butcher's table."

Devin was snapped out of his sick fantasy and back to the task at hand. "Yes, dear. I love you, dear."

"Good. See that you do." Carol closed the door and resumed her place in the kitchen.

The band saw was fitted with a blade that would cut through bone and set atop a roller stand. He rolled it over to the side of his helpless victim. Her arms were splayed out to her sides in a crucifixion pose, and he grabbed the right one. "Here we go, darlin'. Let me know if this tickles." He pushed her right arm through the bandsaw blade, sawing it off just below the elbow.

Her screams and howls were muffled by the tape that, by now, was sprayed with her blood. Her face was a mess of blood, makeup, and tears. All the whimpering in the world wouldn't help her as he made his brutally measured cuts.

By the time he had finished, he had used up a whole box of gallon-sized freezer bags and butcher paper. The meat of the left thigh he kept out of the bags, but rinsed off the blood and brought it in the kitchen, presenting it to Carol like a new piece of jewelry. At last, they would have Thanksgiving dinner.

The End

About the author: Wade CWade Cox was born and raised in Southwest Virginia, in the Roanoke area. For those of you who have no idea where that is, draw an imaginary line between Atlanta and New York City...Roanoke, VA, is the midpoint of that line. His younger brother was a voracious reader, and Wade picked up the habit from him. He wasn't always a writer, but always considered himself a storyteller, from publishing a short story in the library in elementary school to writing short blurbs for fake movies in high school, to the creative writing classes he took in college. His influences range all over from Stephen King to Jimmy Buffett, from detective noir to horror comedy.

My other publications:

I have a few self-published titles available on Amazon Kindle, and the book that I just published is Lost in Paradise, about a traumatized detective who is on the hunt for a missing computer hacker who is on the run from the Russian Mafia.

Uncle Stu's Thanksgiving Turkey

by: Lance Loot

Thanksgiving Day — 1989

The young boy admired himself in the full-length mirror attached to his closet door. With his crisp black pants, white dress shirt adorned with fancy ivory-like buttons, and sleek suspenders, he knew for certain he was going to be the spiffiest looking seven-year-old at his family's annual Thanksgiving get-together.

Never mind the fact that he would be the only seven-year-old in attendance.

The boy couldn't help but beam a toothy smile at his dapper reflection as he straightened his little red bow tie. Truth be told, he looked like a million bucks.

"Hey, c'mere and let me get a good look at my little man all dressed up!" a female voice called out from down the hall.

The boy rolled his eyes—the voice belonged to his mother. She was always treating him like a little kid, always fussing over every minute detail of his appearance. He couldn't wait until he got older and was perceived as more of a big, strong adult rather than a tiny, fragile baby.

"Coming, Mom!" the boy replied, striding down the hallway to his mother's room.

Upon seeing her snazzy son, the mom's face

brightened like a movie marquee.

"Oh, you look so handsome!" she exclaimed, touching the boy's cheek.

"Thanks, Mom..." he muttered, retracting from his mother's touch because he was far too manly for such parental displays of affection.

"I just need to finish blow-drying my hair, then we'll go meet your dad and sister at Grandma's, okay?"

The boy nodded and sauntered toward the kitchen for a quick snack, yanking open the refrigerator door and perusing its contents. The cacophony of his mother's blow dryer blared throughout the house, almost sounding like the agonized bleating of some wounded animal.

A rough knocking at the front door punched through the droning noise; the boy jumped in surprise. He quickly closed the fridge and gaped at the front door, just across the room from him on the opposite wall, then shifted his gaze to the main hallway in the direction of his mother's room.

"Mom? There's someone at the d—"

Another series of knocks came, harder this time, and the boy gasped. The white static of the hairdryer continued—his mother couldn't hear the sharp rapping over the machine's whirring. He stared at the door again. He knew now wasn't the time to be a scared little kid; no, now was the time for him to be the man of the house and answer the door for their visitor. Well, until his mom was available at least.

With a curt nod and a puffing out of his chest, the boy sashayed to the front door and threw it open with purpose.

Nothing, however, could have prepared him for who was on the other side.

Standing outside on the stoop was an absolute mountain of a man, the biggest man the boy had ever seen. He wore a long black overcoat and a wide-brimmed black top hat. His eyes were like two glinting black marbles that seemed to sparkle as they fell upon the boy.

The boy's guts churned into knots, and he had to stifle a yelp as he leaned his head back to meet the leering gaze of the stranger; he felt as if he were looking up at a skyscraper.

"Happy Thanksgiving, young pilgrim," the stranger said, his mouth stretching into a grin and revealing bullet-straight, snow-white teeth.

"Uh... h-happy Thanksgiving..." the boy stammered, his hazel eyes wide and fearful. He swiveled his head back to the hallway, thinking about calling for his mother, but the noisy blow dryer persisted. Reluctantly, he glanced back at the stranger.

"I know, your mother is busy," the stranger said, as if reading the boy's mind. "There is no need to trouble her. You see, I've been watching this house for some time now. You have such a nice, beautiful family, young pilgrim."

He continued to glare at the boy with his oil-black eyes; he still had yet to blink. "I wish I could have a family like yours, but I have no one. I am all alone. So for Thanksgiving, I wish to be part of a nice, beautiful family too, just for one day... just for one holiday dinner. And I want to be a part of your nice, beautiful family, young pilgrim." The stranger's grin expanded unnaturally wider. "What do you say?"

The hair on the back of the boy's neck stood up like quills. "I mean, we're going to my grandma's house soon… to meet—"

"To meet your father and sister," the stranger finished for him. "I know. As I said, I've been watching this house for some time now. I want to join your family for Thanksgiving dinner… if that is alright."

A tense, pregnant silence followed; the stranger continued to stare unblinkingly while grinning, eagerly awaiting a response.

Then it dawned on the boy: the house was quiet again… the blow dryer had shut off! The timing was perfect—as much as he wanted to play the man of the house, this creepy visitor terrified him to his core, and he needed his mother's help.

"I'd have to ask my mom… lemme go get her."

"I understand," the stranger replied. "May I come in while I wait? If it's not too much trouble of course."

The last thing the boy wanted was this man in his house, but it would only be for a minute or two, at least until his mother could take care of business.

"Okay, sure," he said, then raced off in search of his mother. "Mom!"

He almost ran right into her in the middle of the hallway.

"Whoa, watch it!" his mom exclaimed, sidestepping out of the way. "Hey, who were you talking to, honey? I thought I heard voices."

"Mom! There's a scary guy at the door... he said he wants to come to Thanksgiving and he's been watching us and—"

"Wait, what?" she said, her face immediately draining of all color. She raced to the kitchen, the boy following on her heels.

No one was in the kitchen and the front door was wide open.

The mom slammed the door shut and glanced about the room warily. The boy's heartbeat spiked;

he knew something wasn't right.

A sudden, shrill beeping caused them both to cry out in alarm. The mom spun and saw it came from the oven, the beeping signifying it had begun to preheat.

She glanced at her son with dilated pupils. "Stu, why did you touch the oven, you know you're not allowed!"

"I... I didn't..." he replied in a quivering voice.

Her eyes swept the rest of the kitchen, and upon sighting the knife block on the counter, she quickly noticed from an empty slot that the largest one was missing.

"Honey... what did you do with the knife?! Where —"

His mom trailed on, but he didn't hear any of it—he was too focused on something behind her and felt as though his body had turned to ice.

There in the back hallway leading to the laundry room and garage was the stranger, his towering form seemingly materializing from the shadows like a phantom. The whites of his eyes and the teeth of his clenched, too wide grin gleamed through the darkness like moonlight.

"Honey, what is it?" the mom asked, cradling the boy's mortified face. She followed his gaze to the back hallway and screamed.

The stranger lurched into the kitchen, his top hat nearly touching the ceiling, and raised a black-gloved hand clutching a long silver knife—the missing knife from the block. The blade glinted in the room's overhead fluorescent light just before he brought it down violently through the air like a deadly bird of prey, burying the knife to the hilt in the mom's neck with a wet squelching sound, reducing her screaming to choked gurgling. The mom dropped to her knees as her eyes bugged out and pink froth bubbled from her mouth. The stranger yanked the knife from her neck and the mom collapsed to the linoleum, her body twitching.

The boy began hyperventilating as his bladder let go and hot urine streamed down his leg. The stranger lifted his mother's corpse with inhuman strength and placed her face up atop the kitchen island. At that moment, the oven began chirping merrily, announcing it was fully preheated and ready to go. The stranger glanced at the oven, then slowly turned his head and locked eyes with the catatonic boy.

"I hope you're hungry, young pilgrim," he said, smiling like a lunatic.

The stranger plunged the knife into the mother's stomach and began slicing through her flesh as if he were carving a Thanksgiving turkey.

***

Thanksgiving Day — 2023

The table was set for six at the Kent household.

Mountains of mashed potatoes, a smorgasbord of sweet potatoes, a cauldron of green bean casserole, and gaggles of gravy boats ornamented the countertops, all of the food untouched and growing increasingly colder by the minute. Susan and Ryan Kent exchanged annoyed, impatient looks with one another while their two kids

—Hunter and Abbey—sat on the sofa in the adjoining living room, animatedly playing a video game.

The two guests of honor were missing in action, delaying their Thanksgiving feast.

"Stu and Karen comin' or what?" Ryan asked his wife. "Didja try callin' 'em?"

Susan rolled her eyes. "Of course, several times! Both their phones go straight to voicemail."

"Well isn't that great—fashionably late and unresponsive. Plus, Screwy Stuey's still gonna have to cook his precious bird in the oven, setting us back another half hour... whenever they show up..."

"Ryan, what did I tell you about using that horrible name," Susan glowered. She swept a hand in the direction of the living room. "Especially around the kids! They love Stu! They don't need to be hearing you calling their uncle that!"

As if on cue, the kids shrieked in glee from the living room, triggered by a raucous event in their game.

"I don't think you have anything to worry about with that," Ryan replied, side-eyeing his screaming children. "Besides, to be honest… I don't care for your brother, babe. Just something… off about him. I dunno."

"Are you serious right now?" Susan hissed. "How insensitive can you be? Stu and I had a rough childhood—you know what he went through! He was in the behavioral unit for eight goddamn months afterward too! But you're gonna stand there all high and mighty and claim you don't like him because he's endured the worst kind of trauma." She paused, narrowing her eyes to slits. "Real fuckin' nice, Ryan."

"Look, no… all I'm saying is—"

He was interrupted by a powerful barrage of knocks at the door. Then, without warning, it flew open, revealing a tall, lanky guy with wacky dark hair jutting out in all directions as if he had sprouted Medusa's head of snakes. He wore brown slacks with a garish Hawaiian button-up shirt and was balancing a silver platter on one hand. Atop the platter was a large, misshapen object wrapped in tinfoil.

"Yeehaw!" the guy hollered. "Uncle Stu is officially in da' house, family!"

Hunter and Abbey raced into the room, wailing at the top of their lungs, and hugged their uncle. Susan grinned from ear to ear while Ryan grimaced and shrank back further into the kitchen.

"Here, lemme take that for ya!" Susan said, grabbing the platter from her brother and setting it on the kitchen island; she glanced beyond the door's threshold behind Stu, expecting his better half to come traipsing up at any moment. "Hey, where's Karen? Didn't she come, too?"

"Aw, you know how Karen is!" Stu replied while subjecting Hunter to a vigorous noogie. "She had something else she was dying to do! Ah well, her loss, right?" He slung an arm around the shoulder of both Hunter and Abbey and winked at them. "You're just gonna have to settle with your ol' Uncle Stu for this annual T-givin' go-around!"

"Cool with me, Uncle Stu!" Hunter said with a grin.

"Same, you're my favorite uncle!" Abbey added.

"I'm your only uncle, Abbs!" Stu replied with a chuckle. "But I still appreciate the thought!" His manic ice-blue eyes danced about the kitchen and fell on Ryan sulking in the corner. "What's up there, Ry-Ry?! You ready to gorge on delicious comfort food or ya gonna hide out in the shadows all night?"

"I've been ready, Stu. For going on almost an hour now as a matter of—"

"Oh-kay then!" Susan quickly exclaimed, interrupting her husband; she strode to the kitchen island and snatched up Stu's Thanksgiving offering, lifting it by the handles on either side of the platter. "So how long should I put this in the oven for, Stu?"

"Well, let's see… I already pre-cooked my baby back at my place, so… I'd say cook her at 350 for fifteen and we'll check her temp after!"

"Okay! Already got the oven preheated and ready!" Susan said with a smile. She placed the platter on the stovetop and craned her neck to inhale the enticing scent of the foil-wrapped mound. It yielded a heavenly, savory aroma with a lingering smokiness. "Wow! This smells spectacular, Stu! I think you may have outdone yourself this time!" She swiveled to Ryan, who was still brooding in the corner. "Babe, c'mere... you've gotta come smell this!"

Ryan, his mouth a thin line, reluctantly obeyed and plodded over to the oven. However, once the rich, palatable perfume of the concealed loaf crept its way into his nostrils, his bitter demeanor melted away like butter under a flame.

"Holy shit..." he muttered, his eyebrows vaulting to his hairline.

Stu placed his hands on his hips and smirked. "See? Worth the wait, isn't it?"

"I wanna smell too!" Hunter and Abbey chorused, racing to the stove. Susan snickered and carefully brought the platter down to her kids' level so they could each take a turn sniffing.

Ryan wheeled to Stu, finally acknowledging his presence like a normal human being. "Gotta say, that's one tasty-smelling bird, man. You still got that smoker on your property, right?"

"Yes indeedy! Use it for just about everything too! I love a hint of smokiness in any meat! Brings out the flavor, ya know?"

"Listen to master chef Stu over here, revealing his culinary secrets!" Susan chuckled, opening the oven door and sliding the platter inside to bake.

"Cooking is my true passion, Sue!" Stu beamed with a toothy grin. "Anyhow, I gotta share all my best-kept culinary secrets with the family... otherwise, who's gonna carry on Uncle Stu's legacy after I'm dust in the wind?" He swiftly spun toward his niece and nephew with a frenzied glint in his eye. "Right, kiddos?!" He pounced, charging toward them with a roar—the children fled to the living room howling merrily. The chase dead-ended at the sofa, where Stu wrangled both kids, and a boisterous tickle fight ensued. Hunter and Abbey screeched, attempting to finagle out of their uncle's clutches, but Stu held onto them steadfastly.

Susan leaned back against the oven and observed the living room shenanigans with a smile. Even Ryan couldn't help but chortle slightly.

"C'mon babe, help me put everything on the table," Susan said to her husband, springing to action and hoisting nearby bowls of potatoes and corn. "That way we can start eating as soon as Stu's turkey is done."

"Sounds like a plan, I'm freakin' famished!" Ryan replied. He juggled the cauldron of casserole and an overloaded pan of candied yams and arranged them on the table.

Meanwhile, the tides had turned in the tickle fight with Hunter and Abbey joining forces against Stu. He fell back on the sofa, cackling against their relentless assault. "Okay, okay! You guys win, I give! Uncle I say, uncle!"

Giggling, the kids climbed off him, the clear victors of the battle. Stu leaped to his feet, brushed himself off, and stretched. "You guys got me real good there! C'mon, let's go help your mom and dad set up. The sooner the table's set, the sooner we can eat!"

Every member of the Kent family seized a dish or glass of sorts and transported it to the table. Soon, everything was placed, and the oven began trilling gaily to announce the turkey was fully cooked and ready for ravenous consumption.

"Go ahead, sit down everyone! I'll get it!" Stu said as he strode to the oven. Everyone obliged and took their seats as he pulled on a wooly mitt, popped open the door, and extracted his bird. The resulting smell that permeated throughout the room was divine, and the family watched with their mouths watering as Stu brought the glorious turkey to the island and unwrapped its foil casings.

However, once it was unbound and fully revealed, the meaty mound wasn't an actual turkey, although it looked to have been meticulously molded to resemble one. It was an amalgamation of various cuts of meat, each thick slice puzzled together to mimic the shape of a cooked Thanksgiving bird. Wispy steam tendrils coiled from the loaf as Stu began forking generous cutlets onto plates for each family member.

"Uhh, Stu?" Ryan asked, eyeing the "turkey" on the island with suspicion. "What exactly is that? Thought you were cookin' us a bird?"

"I know, I know!" Stu exclaimed while making the rounds around the table, placing a helping of the meat in front of each Kent. "But consider this my unique spin on a classic! Just trust me and give it a try—you're gonna go crazy for it, I promise!"

Susan—fork, and knife in hand at the ready—studied the meat before her, then frowned at her brother warily. "Stu…? Are you…? Did you…?" She trailed off as she struggled to formulate into words the burgeoning questions her mind yearned to ask.

Ryan stared at the sizable slice in front of him, leery of trying a bite. But as its luscious, tantalizing aroma kissed his olfactory senses, he dismissed any reservations and tore off a chunk, shoving it into his eager mouth. The texture of the meat was absolute perfection, instantaneously melting in his mouth. And the taste? It was every bit as breathtakingly delicious as the smells had hinted at and more. The full-bodied flavor assaulted his palate, stimulating and igniting each taste bud like a kaleidoscopic fireworks display. Ryan's eyes rolled back into his head from the sheer ecstasy of the meat's essence. His body tingled as though every nerve was in a state of fiery rapture.

All the while, the rest of his family analyzed him with curious wonder. Stu, still hovering at the edge of the table, scrutinized Ryan's reaction with rapt focus like a scientist studying a three-headed cat.

A low moan escaped Ryan's lips as he came out of his reverie. Then, realizing there was plenty more where that came from, began shoveling the rest of his "turkey" into his salivating jowls. The other Kents, swayed by Ryan's elation as well as the delectable odors wafting in front of their faces, also began consuming their "turkey" portions, each of them quickly experiencing their blissful epiphanies from the meat's godlike flavor sensations. Soon, all of the Kents were leaping from their seats and dashing to the silver platter for seconds, thirds, and even fourth helpings. The rest of the myriad food dishes on the table were left completely untouched.

Stu observed them devour his "turkey" like a pack of malnourished bears fresh out of hibernation. He smiled as his heart swelled with joy.

This was the perfect Thanksgiving he had always dreamed of: his whole family in one place enjoying the hell out of his masterpiece, his culinary magnum opus.

"So..." Stu said with a toothy smirk. "Thoughts? Whatcha guys think?! C'mon, I want all the details!"

Ryan took a moment to swallow his huge mouthful. "Hell, man. This is easily the best meal I've ever had in my life..." He immediately returned to scarfing down his portions.

Hunter and Abbey, their mouths loaded beyond capacity, replied with unintelligible murmurs of high praise.

Susan stared at her cleared plate and said nothing.

Stu turned his lamp-like gaze upon her. "Hey,

don'cha want more there, Sue? Still some left!"

She smiled faintly. "Thanks, but I'm beyond stuffed, Stu. I don't think I could eat another bite…"

"Oh c'mon, have some more! After all, we can't leave any uneaten! She wouldn't want any part of her going to waste, especially giving us meat this scrum diddly-sumptuous!"

As Susan watched her family continue to consume the final remnants of the "turkey," she thought deeper into what her brother had just said; a horrible thought began bubbling to the surface from the darkest recesses of her brain.

"Stu…" she started, her voice a quavering whisper. "When you say 'she wouldn't want any part of her going to waste,' you don't mean… you can't mean…" She paused as a heinous memory, one she had repressed for decades, slowly swirled into focus in her mind's eye. She gaped at her brother, her face pure white, drained of all color.

"…where is Karen really, Stu?"

Stu met her panicked gaze, his ice-blue eyes shimmering as he smiled like a lunatic.

"Oh, Sue... don't tell me after all these years you haven't been at least a little curious about the taste..." he replied slyly.

Susan could only stare at the licked-clean plate in front of her as the awful memory swam into view and commandeered her consciousness. The rest of the Kent family paid her no mind as they ate up the last scraps of Stu's Thanksgiving "turkey."

***

Thanksgiving Day — 1989

"I just wanna check why Mommy isn't answering the phone real quick, then I promise we'll go right back to Grandma's, okay?" the dad said to his daughter, holding her hand and leading her to the front door of their house.

"Okay," the little girl—five-year-old Susan—replied.

The dad went to put his key in the lock, but as he pushed on the door, it creaked open on its own—it hadn't been fully closed.

"What the..." the dad started.

Upon seeing the ghastly bloodbath inside, a low moan escaped his agape mouth and he fell to his knees. Susan, her young mind unable to process what she was seeing exactly, could only look about the place in wide-eyed confusion.

The room looked more like a slaughterhouse than a kitchen. What was left of the mom's ragged, dismembered body was laid out on the kitchen island. Her mangled corpse hardly resembled what could have once been considered human, more like giant pulpy bits of blood orange.

But that wasn't even the worst part.

Seven-year-old Stu sat cross-legged beside the island on the gore-stained linoleum. His once snazzy outfit was completely soaked through with his mother's blood. Clutched in his small hands was an enormous slab of cooked meat, meat that had once been part of his mother's body. Stu's crimson-spattered face was devoid of any expression, save for the foggy, dreamlike quality misting within his eyes as he continued to absentmindedly eat his mom bit by bit.

The End

About the author: Whether creating at-home comics or opus-like stories, a lifelong love of all things eldritch and macabre brought Lance to writing. Taking inspiration from daily life and distorting it like a funhouse mirror for your reading enjoyment is what he does best.

Lance lives in a centenarian haunted house in Illinois with his wife and three cats.

Published Works:

Scrapyard Shuffle

Link: https://godless.com/products/scrapyard-shuffle-by-lance-loot-emerge-18?_pos=1&_sid=bfa609148&_ss=r

The Tick Tock Man (Descent into Madness anthology)

Link: https://www.amazon.com/DESCENT-INTO-MADNESS-ENTER/dp/B0CJ465JQZ/ref=sr_1_3?

crid=28M0HVTJV62YO&keywords=descent+into
+madness&qid=1698708717&sprefix=descent
+into+madnes%2Caps%2C108&sr=8-3

Deadhead Ride Down the Cemetery Lane (Halloweenthology anthology)

Link: https://www.lulu.com/shop/parth-sarathi-chakraborty/halloweenthology-d%C3%ADa-de-muertos/paperback/product-84zw7y7.html?page=1&pageSize=4#product-reviews

"The Contributor"

by

ALLISHA MCADOO

Chase Will

The dining room table is set for four people: Me, Papa, Mama, and Nana. It feels like so long since the previous Thanksgiving dinner; time drags by in our family, living so far from civilization on a private farm without neighbors to pass the days with. It gets so lonely out here that some days I think I would do anything just for a friend. But I'm not allowed to have friends. Papa says outsiders are dangerous, which is why our family is self-sustaining.

The turkey's in the kitchen oven, and we all sit in the next room over. The table cover is crimson with little cornucopias decorating it, and a great big candle sits in the center of the empty table, illuminating the empty white room. We've spent all afternoon unplugging appliances around the house and removing everything but the table from the dining room—electricity somehow disrupts the process, Papa says, and we need all the room we can get for it to work well.

    Flies make tiny shadows over Nana's face

as they hover around her. There's still dirt in the cracks of her face and beneath her fingernails. It took great pains for her to be here tonight, and she no doubt brought her appetite.

Papa stares down at the festive orange and brown doily beneath his glass of red wine. He fidgets mindlessly with the tablecloth with his left hand while we all wait in silence for dinner to begin.

Mama sets an empty white platter on the table beside a large and serrated carving knife. She's in close proximity to Nana as she does this, and she seems to be holding her breath as if it will help with the stench. She doesn't dare cover her mouth or show the stinging tears filling her eyes. That would be an insult to Nana, and Nana's not one to be disrespected.

Candlelight dances around Nana's vacant expression, and for the briefest moment, it's as if she's still alive.

Papa stands. He lifts his empty wine glass with his left hand and clears his throat.

"Today is a day of gratitude," he begins. "Gratitude for life. For family. For what waits beyond this world for true believers."

He looks at Nana. Her skin is dried up and papery-looking. She's been dead for six years now, but her flesh has never rotted, and the worms in our backyard don't dare feast upon her. She never misses Thanksgiving feasts, because it's the one time each year we rely fully on her. Brownish drool runs down her chin as she turns her head just the slightest bit and looks at me, her favorite granddaughter.

"Thanksgiving is also a time to remember sacrifice," Papa continues. "There's nothing in this world more important than family, and there's no limit to what we sacrifice for those we love."

Papa reaches for the knife with his left hand. The little nub of his pinky finger always makes me uneasy. But I think of why we're here and how much this celebration means to us all. It's the biggest day of the year for us, and I can't be distracted by something as silly as Papa's missing finger.

And this year it's my turn to contribute.

"Before we feast," Papa continues, "let us pray. Join hands please."

Mama reaches her left hand toward me. Her pinky finger is also missing, and I do my best not to touch the nub as I gently take her hand. Her finger's only been missing for one year, unlike Papa, whose pinky's been missing for two years. I've had plenty of time to get used to it, though. I need to grow up; it's time to be an adult, finally, and not let little changes make me uncomfortable.

Papa takes my other hand, and he puts his arm around Nana's living corpse. We close our eyes.

"Our Lord R'yual," he begins. "Thank you for another bountiful year away from society and all its evils and corruption. Our crops have bloomed time and time again, and our livestock has provided hearty nutrition to keep us strong. Thank you for allowing Nana to join us once more. We pray that our sacrifice keeps her strong in the ground for another year. In your name we pray.

Amen."

"Amen," Mama and I repeat in unison.

Then Papa lifts the knife to eye level. Candlelight dances off the blade as he brings it to Nana's right ear. He barely has to saw at the flesh; the ear peels away from her skull with ease as soon as the serrated teeth touch her flesh. He sets the knife back down and holds the ear overhead in both hands.

"Today marks an important point in our tradition," he says. "Today, my daughter transcends from childhood to the life of a contributor. Mama and I are both proud to see her blossom into a young and responsible woman."

Mama motions for me to stand up, smiling as Papa lowers Nana's ear. I take my place at Papa's side, and I open my mouth for communion.

"Eat this, for it is the flesh of our Lord R'yual," he instructs, placing the dirt-covered ear on my tongue.

I chew slowly, trying not to wince at the disgusting taste. I want to make Papa and Mama proud.

And then Papa puts the knife to Nana's wrist, making a quick and deep horizontal slash between two similar markings. Inky black blood drips toward the floor in a slow stream. Nana's been dead for so long that there shouldn't be any blood left in her corpse, but there it is, clear as day. It's just how things work in our family, I suppose. If I had friends, I would ask them if they have similar traditions in their family, traditions they don't fully understand but participate in nonetheless.

Papa holds the empty wine glass beneath the stream of blood, collecting it until the glass is half-filled. He lifts the glass momentarily toward the ceiling, and then he presents it to me.

"Drink this, for it is the blood of our Lord R'yual," he says.

He places the glass to my lips, and I drink deeply. I immediately want to throw up. It tastes like rotten meat, even worse than Nana's dead flesh. But I don't even gag; I drink the entire glass and then I smile at Papa gladly. I'm doing so well. It's almost over…just one more step.

Papa smiles. I haven't seen his eyes light up like this in a long time, and it makes me so happy that I momentarily stop thinking about what comes next.

Then Papa picks up the knife again.

"And now," he says, "present your left hand, and become a contributing member of our family."

I'm hesitant to offer my hand. Every bone in my body rebels against the idea, and I think of all the blood on the table when Papa cut off his finger last year. I think of the look of pain on his face, and Nana's ear-to-ear smile as she accepted the offering into her mouth and swallowed it whole.

But then I think of how the family depends on me. The same member of the family can't contribute twice until we've gone a full rotation, at least according to Papa, so I have to be the one to make the sacrifice. Without my sacrifice, Nana doesn't eat. And if Nana doesn't eat, she won't survive in the ground for another year. And without Nana's living corpse in the fields, our corn won't grow, and R'yual will curse our livestock to famine.

I put my left hand on the table and spread my fingers wide. Papa sets the blade on my pinky.

"I'm proud of you," he says quietly. "Remember that."

And then he slams his other hand onto the top of the blade, severing flesh and bone in an instant, and it's all over before I can even cry out. The pain is tremendous, but I don't scream; I don't even make a sound. I'm brave, just like Mama and Papa want me to be.

Papa picks up the severed finger and holds it to Nana's lips. Her black tongue extends from her mouth, and Papa places the finger on it. Her jaw moves slowly up and down as she chews.

Mama and Papa watch her closely, waiting with nervous expressions. Any moment, Nana will swallow the finger, nod her head slowly, and then walk back to the field to crawl back under the dirt for another year. My hand is throbbing in pain, and

I feel tears welled up in my eyes. I don't let Mama and Papa see me cry, however. Twelve-year-olds aren't supposed to act like babies.

But then Nana makes a sound I've never heard from her before, and she falls forward in her seat, thrashing about violently as she tears at her throat.

She's choking on my finger!

"Help her!" Mama cries, standing up so quickly she rattles the table.

Papa is behind Nana in an instant, arms locked around her chest and heaving against her. Nothing comes out of her mouth but more of the strange noises. They're not choking sounds; it's as if she's trying to speak a dozen languages at once without success.

Then she flies backward in her seat, nearly knocking Papa over. Her glassy dead eyes are wide now, and she points an accusatory finger at me.

"Y...you..." she says.

And then she collapses forward onto the

table, absolutely still and silent now.

Mama screams.

"Is she...gone?" Papa asks, picking her corpse up from the table and leaning her back in her seat again. "Maybe this was supposed to happen," he says desperately. "Maybe it's just part of the ritual we haven't seen yet, or..."

He trails off, and I think of Nana's final gesture. The way she pointed at me. I feel tears finally run down my cheeks as I try to catch my breath. I've failed Mama and Papa. Somehow, I've failed at such a simple task.

And then the candle flickers out, and the four of us are in total darkness.

Two red orbs appear where Nana's eyes were, illuminating her wrinkled face. I see black smoke coming from between her lips as she speaks.

"It is over," she says. Only it isn't her voice; something else is speaking through her like a pupped, something with a low and growly voice. Her demonic red eyes settle on me. "The final sacrifice is complete. You've done my bidding well, young one. You and your family will survive what comes next."

And then Nana's head cranes backward, and like smoke from a chimney, black ooze shoots from her mouth, spraying off the ceiling and showering us all. The stream remains steady for a long moment before Nana's lifeless body slumps forward again in her seat. The three of us remain still, covered in the foul black goo.

A bright light from outside shines in through the kitchen window, and all at once I get a strong whiff of smoke, the same kind as when Mama left the turkey in the oven for too long when I was an even smaller child, back before Nana died at we started with the sacrifices to R'yual.

Papa rushes to the window, and I see a bright orange light dancing off his empty expression.

"What is it?" Mama asks, rushing to his side. "What do you see?"

Except I already know what it is. Fire...the

world is on fire. And it's all my fault.

Papa looks at me, devastation on his face.

"What have you done?" he asks. "Where did you go wrong?"

I think of the Thanksgiving turkey on the kitchen table, the turkey that smelled so good after a long day of preparatory starvation. How was I supposed to stop myself when I noticed neither Papa nor Mama were watching me? It was only one bite. A single early bite from the moist and delicious meat couldn't have caused all this...could it?

Papa doesn't wait for me to answer. He rushes from the room, and Mama and I both follow. He stands at the front door for a moment, bracing himself as he wraps his hand in the bottom of his button-up shirt and then touches the hot handle. Light from the flames outside is lighting up the entire room now. It's as if the sun is out again, right outside our window.

Then he opens the door, and I see the true carnage I've caused.

The fields are a blazing furnace, and I see escaped animals from our barn running aflame through the front yard: pigs, chickens, and turkeys...all engulfed in flame.

And then I see him, lifting one great black hand from within the flame toward the night sky.

Our Lord R'yual has risen.

All because of one bite.

The End

About the author: Chase Will is the author of Mandated Smiles and Other Strange Tales and Where Dreams Are Entombed. He can be found at www.ChaseWill.com

When Black Friday Comes - by Jack Presby

Grant took one more forkful of pumpkin pie and then pushed the plate away. He picked up his coffee cup and went over to the percolator for a fresh cup. He hated those Mr. Coffee machines with a passion and forgot about a Keurig. Trash as far as he was concerned. Good, old-fashioned brewed coffee was the way to go. And nothing brewed one better than a percolator. He stood there for a moment, savoring the aroma and enjoying the warmth of the mug in his hands. The perfect end to a perfect meal. He surveyed the living room and smiled. Family. All the people he loved were gathered here together for Thanksgiving. The voice of his wife brought him back from wherever his brain was wandering.

"Hello? Grant? Are you there?"

"Sorry love. Just enjoying the moment while I can."

"Your father seems to be having a great time."

"My father and football. His mistress," Grant said and laughed a little.

"So, I was thinking maybe we could go out into the yard and build a fire. Have after-dinner drinks and cigars. What do you think?"

"Sorry Monica, I have to leave for work. Tomorrow is Black Friday, you know it starts our busy season."

"I know, but, could you go in a little later? After all, it's only five-thirty."

A voice from the living room broke the moment.

"Grant, get in here and settle a bet would you please," said his father.

"Coming pop," Grant said.

Grant walked into the living room. His

father was sitting in his favorite spot, the center sofa. His arms were waving wildly as he was trying to make his point. He noticed Grant and said,

"Good. My boy is here. Grant, help settle a bet with my brother. Remember Fred Lane?"

"The Panthers running back," said Grant.

"Yes. Remember how he died?"

"Of course. His wife shot him."

His father laughed and then held out his hand.

"OK, losers, pay up. I told you Grant would know. If there's a death involved, Grant's the authority."

Grant smiled and shook his head. He looked at his uncles and nephews gathered in the living room and said his goodbyes. He told them he had to leave for work and that they should feel free to stay as long as they wanted. Or at least until the beer ran out.

Grant stopped at the closet, took out a black

cloak, and put it on. He reached into the back and pulled out a walking stick. After closing the door, he checked his reflection in the mirror. Satisfied, he smiled and walked over to his wife.

"OK Monica, I'm leaving," Grant said as he embraced her.

"Are you sure you have to leave?"

"Maybe I'll get lucky and get done early. But no promises."

Grant kissed Monica and told her that he loved her. Then he left for work.

Grant walked up to the newsstand located at the bus terminal and bought a newspaper and a Clark Bar. Then he walked over to the kiosk for the Route fifteen bus and sat on a bench. He opened the newspaper to the obituaries and folded it so that it was now the top page. Then he opened the Clark Bar and settled in for his wait. Route fifteen was a few minutes late when it finally arrived at the kiosk. Grant got up and got in the back of the queue. He boarded the bus swiped his pass and looked for an empty seat. He was in luck. There was one seat open next to a mousey-looking woman and he took it. He continued to read the paper and snack on the candy while the bus made its first stops. He could sense the woman looking at him, so he glanced at her and smiled. She was thin and rough-looking. Her brown hair was cut severely and he noticed tape holding her glasses together at one temple. She smiled back and then gave a half turn in his direction.

"Happy Thanksgiving," she said.

Grant nodded politely and smiled.

"Happy Thanksgiving," he replied.

"This is a special Thanksgiving for me. It's my first one clean and sober in ten years. I don't mind telling you how good it feels to be almost normal. Although, I'll never really be normal again. See, I'm an addict. Oh, it's not like you think. I wasn't a joy popper. See, I got injured at work. Hurt my back badly. And back then, all the workman s comp doctors used to do was give you Oxy's. And naturally, once the damage was done, they cut you off the painkillers and force you to hit the streets. At first, it was just some Percocets here and there. Then they got really expensive and I found out heroin was cheaper. At first, I just snorted it. Just a little. Then smoking it, and then finally, the spike. You might not realize it when you look at me, but I used to have a decent body. I was in a long-term relationship that was close to marriage, but the heroin took all my time. When I wasn't stoned, I was working on my next purchase. I was mugged and robbed more times than I'd like to admit. I was victimized by so-called friends I met in my first recovery program. If you ever want really good drugs, go to a rehab. I learned so much about the way of the junkie that it became my life. I finally reached rock bottom when I discovered that my boyfriend was cheating on me with two other women. After I confronted him, he made me realize how unhappy I've been making him. How we weren't a couple like we were. How we no longer could go out or do anything normal because my life was tied to the spike. I felt betrayed. I had no other world to live in. My family long ago disowned me. Barely speaking to me and only during the holidays. I missed weddings and funerals. Baptisms. I missed my nieces and nephews growing up. I missed a lot of life. Finally, my boyfriend confronted me. If I didn't get my act together and clean up, I was out on the street. Well, I don't mind telling you it shook me. So I worked on getting into a program. It took three tries to finally find one that was right. That was six months ago. I gradually got off the heroin, with a lot of help. And now, here I am going to work for the first time in almost ten years."

She paused. Took a deep breath and then continued.

"I'm awfully sorry to be rambling on like this. Especially to a stranger on the bus. But, I'm so happy right now I can't help myself. So, tell me about you. Are you going to visit someone?"

"I'm headed to work too," said Grant. Then he put the hood of his cloak up over his head. The change was subtle, but the young woman saw it. She saw Grant's skin become transparent. She was able to see his skull and the bones in his hand holding the walking stick. And the walking stick. It seemed to double in length and take on the appearance of a scythe.

A man sitting in front of them rose and pulled a Kabar knife out from the inside of his coat. He turned so that he was facing the young woman and looked her in the eyes.

"Death becomes you," he said as he swung the Kabar in an arc that caught her in the left temple and pinned her head to the bus window. Blood poured from her mouth as she tried to speak, but only gurgled and sputtered. The woman sitting behind her screamed first, then she was joined by others screaming to stop the bus and to call the police.

Grant removed his hood and his appearance changed back. When the bus stopped, he got off and started to walk towards home. Looks like I got done work early, he thought, Monica will be so pleased.

The End

About the author Jack Presby:

Already having written for the stage and screen, Jack's first published story was in the anthology Luckier Than You (an extreme horror anthology). He has Heart of the Mavka and Mama and the Mavka Out, a collaboration written with Allisha McAdoo. The Mavka collection can be found in paperback on Amazon. All e-books are found on Godless, Pubshare, Apple Books, Nook, Kobo, Goodreads, and Kindle. Jack Presby and Allisha McAdoo also released a short story collaboration called Twisted Images.

When not writing, Jack can be found looking for exotic recipes to serve where he cooks.

You can follow Jack on all social platforms.

Facebook: www.Facebook.com/Jack.presby

Twitter: @jackpresby

Instagram: jackpresby

CRANBERRY SAUCE

BY

JASON GEHLERT

The vast dining room offered parallel rows of seated guests. A tightened atmosphere, elbow to elbow, thick stale heated air, and a lengthy festive holiday tablecloth of a hungered appetite. To draw another example, the sturdy legs of the dormant chairs rubbed their oak wood against each other like dogs in heat.

The host, a wiry, highly intelligent professor of anthropology at the local community college, clasped his slender oily fingers. His darkened slide into middle age disturbed him.

The friction of resisting aging was unrelenting. A man of high hopes, his dreams were ultimately dashed many times over. No one took him seriously. They mocked him and his curious methods. The student body mocked his cavalier and pretentious appearance. The pewter thin wire frame glasses, cheeks pocked with small circles from a childhood disease, and uneven fingers that were jaundiced from aggressive chain-smoking gas station cigarettes.

His steady left hand scraped the small strips of meat across his family dinnerware. The scraping of metal against the expensive chinaware didn't stir any response from his dinner guests. His uneven teeth ground the meat to bits, all the while his steady right hand brought the clear crystalized wine glass to his pursed, chapped lips.

A deep red painted his lips as he swallowed the tart liquid.

He was mesmerized by his mind's cautious plans for this special dinner. The gallery of guests was hand-picked, with their array of unique minds and talents. His scraped right hand gently placed the wine glass down and caught a pesky fly between his grimy fingers. The soft crunching of the fly's exoskeleton brought him joy. More flies danced around the room. The chandelier lights waned and dimmed, clinging to their last wattage.

The fork gripped the strip of meat. He curled the spaghetti-like substance and slurped it inside his waiting maw. The buttery juices slid down his chin and stained his salt-and-pepper beard. He used his fingers to lick off the rest of the savory scent.

The family portraits hung with pride around the room. All four walls teemed with yesteryear's glory days. An uncle who excelled at hunting held the sought-after trophy. The head of its prey, eyes frozen in fear, and its spinal cord dangling from its cleaved, severed neck. The bloodied tinge of the portrait added to the regality of it all. The uncle's uneven grin would bring uneasiness to many. His filthy, oily, slicked-back coal-black hair was even worse. His left hand held the prey toward the viewer like his main trophy kill. The best example would be the Predator movies and the alien's vast trophy case of worthy kills.

In another vile portrait, our host, all about ten years old, witnessed the horrific slaying of death, scattered within a vast field, or perhaps a meadow. His back was turned to the viewer, as was his father's. The two held hands clasped and interlocked in unrefuted love. Before them, lay severed cherry-colored limbs, rotting heads, and mounds of flesh with flies buzzing in gouged-out eye sockets, and busted ribcages hugging the earth with fear.

Clearing his raspy, hot lungs, a pocket of puce-colored phlegm expunged across the well-worn tablecloth. "Ladies and gentlemen." He raised the wine glass with victory. His left hand reverberated the fork against the family heirloom. "Many of you offer wild theories, sensualized stories, and even downright lies about my character, career, and personal life." He smiled with acute distaste for his guests. A piece of firm al dente-type pasta twisted around one of his jagged, uneven teeth His tongue clacked and slurped more wine. "Barton, my dear, aged, defunct partner." His tone dropped, a snickering baritone of ominous pleasure. "What have you to say about our new project?"

The host became increasingly infuriated and let loose his emotional tirade. "Well! You haven't much to say tonight, hmm?" His fingers twirled the fork and jabbed the bulbous piece of pink meat on his plate. His eyes had a certain wonderful gaze that was focused on Barton's chair. His former partner, now straddled dead in his chair, only held up with the firmest of rope. A mouth agape with a broken jawbone and a tongue that was dismounted with the tender loving care of an aggressive steak knife. "What words may you dispel from that sinister hole of yours!"

His teeth chewed on the tongue with erotic frenzy. The droplets of blood and juice splattered on the plate below. "All of you will remember my name during this hearty Thanksgiving feast!"

"Dr. Ander Willows!" His voice vehemently beamed. "My iconic legacy is now intact." His black, beady eyes glared about the room. "How's karma treating everyone now?" He sneered. "I'd ask good ol' Barton, but he's working on non-verbal communication skills right now."

A snickering bellow soon followed.

"Barton, your warm body will soon become a footnote in the pages of history. It pleases me knowing your hard work will dissolve quicker than lye to flesh." Willows took a hard sip from the glass. "Even the blood of my guests tastes divine against my sinned lips."

A short pause ensued. Willows let the beautiful silence and stench of the room soak in. "A table full of eager guests, all cherry-picked from my little black book of liars, cheaters, and double-crossing cunt sucking douchebags."

"We lead the group with my now former partner, Barton, a man whose unusual gift of gab has certainly become the undoing of his existence." Willows raised a congratulatory toast to Barton. "To a bleak future and rotting flesh." After another sip, his attention turned to a pair of wealthy benefactors who stymied his projects. "And to my middle-aged, rich cocksucker and his twat trophy wife, Lucas, and Veronica, I not only have extracted your entire bank accounts," Willows paused for a brief glimmer of victory, "but, I have also removed the one thing you never had, and never displayed during our partnership." Willows pushed around a bowl filled with a creamy noodle-type substance with the edges of his fork. His hands reached for the condiments. "Hanson," he asked of another guest, "may you pass the pepper?"

Willows laughed as he reached forward. "I mean if you had hands, I'm sure you would." The dark pools of blood at Hanson's place-setting displayed the unrelenting horror that Willow had displayed. Hanson's head was slumped cold dead in his minestrone dish, his arms still resting atop the tablecloth. His diamond-encrusted Rolex rested in its pool of soupy blood. A patch of wavy black hair floated with the chilled soup.

"That's what you get when you plagiarize my work, asshole." Willows forced Hanson's head further into the soup bowl, bobbing the head like a cork. "As for your inadequate parents over there," said Willows, "I'm about to gnaw down on their guts." He peppered the dish with seasoning.

He slurped the intestines with delight. They dangled and slapped against his chin. He stared down the couple, their faces frozen from the atrocious act of their host removing their intestines while they were still awake. Death had taken their souls about an hour earlier.

"Wow, this feast has been tremendous." Willows giggled. He rose and wiped his mouth with a blood-soaked napkin. "While all of this has been appetizing of sorts, I've been waiting impatiently for the main course." He walked by Barton's chair and snapped his neck with a clean twist. He reached down and scooped up Hanson's watch. He slipped it on his right wrist. "It's still ticking." He looked over at the dead parents. "You did have great taste." He pointed to the watch. "I'm afraid that all of you will miss the main course." He glanced at the Rolex. "These diamonds sure are glittery."

A loud knock rapped on the mansion door. Willows walked across the foyer to answer the guest's arrival. His penny loafers squished fading bloodied bodily fluid footprints across the black and white tiled floor. The brass crystalized chandelier swung with perfect precision, as Willows walked underneath it to answer the door. A man of meticulous design, the light bulbs were never choked with dust.

Willows greeted his guest. "Good evening, Dean Chalmers," he said with a grin. "How's your night?

The gruff demeanor of Addison Chalmers had always rubbed the university the wrong way. He was the man. He was the main artery of the entire program. Everything flowed through him. His brown, dusty eyes peered down on Willows. "Professor," his tone was uninviting "For what nuisance of a night am I expecting?"

"Oh," Willows said with a slick smirk. "I have a holiday feast planned for everyone essential to my work and projects."

"It must be a tiny group." Chalmers walked inside and stood firm in the foyer. "What is that abhorrent scent?"

"Oh, that?" Willows came off as sheepish. "My cooking isn't the best."

"Neither is your work."

"Let's just move on to the dinner and allow me to bathe you in adjectives and whimsical stories of yesteryear."

"The only reason I'm here is because the wife is a bore." Chalmers walked through the doorway and into the dining room.

Willows closed the double sliding doors behind the two men.

The room was dark and dank. The relentless stench of blood, urine, and heat stoked the nostrils of Dean Chalmers. His jerking eyes flapped open. His hands were tied to the chair, his ankles as well. His legs spread open and he was stripped down to his naked underwhelming penis. His fair skin was soaked in wetness; the tip of his cock was still hot from the escape of a fearful urine. "What is the meaning of this!"

Willows walked closer. "Meaning of what? Thanksgiving?" He tapped his chin with the crisp, serrated blade of a hunting knife. "It's a holiday of giving back appreciation to those who deserve it."

"I'll call the police."

"No, you won't."

"Why not?" Chalmers became angrier by the second.

Willows slapped him hard. His hand twirled the knife and then stabbed the penis clean into the chair.

A girlish scream erupted from Chalmers. His body quivered and convulsed. His chortled cries were loud and he drooled in anger from his mouth.

With a clean flick, Willows had not only removed the penis but mutilated it so bad, Chalmers would never fuck or procreate again.

The stomping of his feet delighted Willows. "You are a weak man under all that false bravado. And, a weak man without the balls to stand up for one of his own when they come under scrutiny." Willows took the tip of the knife, with strips of penis caught in the serrated blades, and continued to saw and sever the testicles.

Chalmers stirred in his chair. His wrists numbed and gnawed from the ropes; his ankles were as well. His groin still throbbed from the brutality of the act. An act, he had hoped was a nightmare. Yet, for him, this nightmare was real.

A quiet humming Chalmers could sense the nig the brisk breeze from the northern scuffling of a chair's legs snapped his dead center. His eyes watered and weary, the image into focus.

Willows was straddling the chair like crazed lap dancer.

Chalmer's ears ringed with the sound of Willow's hands massaging something. It was a sloshing, slippery noise—a squishing sound.

"So," Willows began. He stared down his boss. "We have some logistical stuff to work out. A transfer of legal power," he paused. "You know, mumbo jumbo type stuff." He opened his right palm. His fingers rolled around two objects that resembled medium-sized dates. "You know in countries testicles are a sought-after dish." grinning disturbed Chalmers. "Thankfully, s will never be."

He swallowed one with a hearty gulp. "It kind of slides right down the ol' esophagus."

Chalmers was speechless.

"Good, good," said Willows, as he swallowed the second testicle. Gulping down hard, his jovial manner continued. "This should be a quick meeting."

The End

About the author: Gehlert edited the anthology Read Us or Die for Black Bed Sheet Books. He is currently prepping the release of several new works.

Armed with a Communication/Media Degree from

SUNY-New Paltz, Gehlert continues to tour the country, from the Playboy Mansion to various horror conventions, offering advice about writing, marketing, and the promotional side of being an author, Jason is conquering the world with his fiction even as you read this. He lives in New York with his golden retriever Jasper and his daughters. Gehlert is an advocate for Down syndrome awareness.

Have Some Turkey
By
Allisha McAdoo

2023 will be a Thanksgiving that no one will ever forget. The month of November was awful and while that is no excuse for what I did, I have no regrets. After Halloween, I lost my job. Apparently telling the customers I don't make the prices and to take their complaints to headquarters was rude. My boss called me into the back hallway. We pretended it was an office. "Crystal, I am sorry but corporate wants to fire you for being rude to customers." His expression was blank as I handed him my badge. I walked out of the store flipping off the cameras and rolling my eyes. I went home thinking everything was going to be ok. At least my husband and I had savings. It would be enough to tide us over until I found a better job. I married my husband Kris shortly after we graduated high school. We have been married now for twenty-three years. Although it wasn't always a happy marriage it was nice to have someone through all of life's trials and tribulations.

The next hour, I went to the bank. "I'm sorry Crystal, your accounts have been emptied." The teller looked uncomfortable. "Can I see a statement of my purchase history for my accounts? Also, can you tell me if Kris took out the money or if bill collectors drained it?" My voice came out as a hoarse whisper. The last time I checked my accounts I had over 200,000 in each account. "Yes, ma'am I'll print out the summaries and check the cameras." She quickly left. I was starting to shake. This couldn't be right. Something must have glitched. I took a deep breath trying to steady my nerves. A few minutes later the teller returned with a stack of papers. " According to the cameras, your husband cleaned out the accounts on August 12th." She said quietly, handing me the paperwork and a screenshot of my husband taking the money. "Thank you for letting me know." I did my best to smile at the teller as I walked away. I did my best to walk out of the bank keeping my composure.

Once back in the car, however, I read over the statements with tears running down my face. My husband of twenty-three years had been slowly withdrawing money out of the savings account and then my account for months now. By the time he cleared out the accounts, there wasn't much left. What pissed me off the most, was the day he cleaned out the accounts, was my birthday. He had told me he was at a conference for the entire week of my birthday. I had spent my birthday alone. He didn't even bother to call me and wish me a happy birthday. He had said that he worked at the conference all day and then fell asleep by six p.m. Looking over the bank statements it was clear that Kris had a mistress. He was paying all her bills, and buying her expensive things. With my money, the money I had worked so hard for all my life. I was now past the point of being angry.

I drove to the property listed on my bank accounts receiving a monthly payment. It was a nice apartment complex. I saw Kris with his arm around a nice-looking blonde woman. They looked happy as they kissed before going into the apartment. Kris was supposed to be at work so why was he with his whore? I called Kris's work pretending I needed to know when his lunch hour was so I could bring him lunch. I was informed Kris hadn't worked at that company in over a year. A year. A whole year of him sponging off of me without telling me. I went back home fuming. In the last 24 hours, I had lost my job, found out my husband was cheating on me, that he hadn't worked in over a year, and took all my money. I wanted to exact revenge. I wanted to hurt Kris.

I paced the house trying to figure out what I wanted to do. I called several attorneys but every single one of them wouldn't be back into the office until after Thanksgiving. My parents were both dead and all I had for family was my estranged brother. I had no other place to go, no job, and my marriage was destroyed. I had two more weeks before Thanksgiving. Then an idea struck me. I knew exactly what I wanted to do for my revenge.

For the next two weeks, I worked odd jobs so I would have enough money to buy what I needed for the Thanksgiving dinner no one would ever forget. Kris pretended to be tired from work and slept on his days off. I pretended everything was ok, and that I didn't know of his indiscretions. We kept up with the appearance of being happily married. I threw myself into every odd job I could find. The thing about temporary jobs is that they suck. One day I would clean up fire damage in rich people's homes, the next day I was scrubbing toilets. Each job seemed to suck just a little bit more than the one before. I was only qualified for shitty jobs. I couldn't land a nice office job despite having plenty of experience.

I began to sell off things I knew that Kris wouldn't notice if it went missing. I didn't trust the bank to not give Kris access to my accounts so I kept all the money I earned on my person at all times. It was embarrassing to have to tell the bank the person I trusted for twenty-three years could no longer be trusted. I had to keep up with appearances because no one could find out how I was buried under rock bottom. Especially since my revenge was important to me, no one could know anything was wrong.

With each temporary job, I managed to steal something that I would need for Thanksgiving dinner. The day before Thanksgiving I began to cook. The house smelled delicious. Kris was being sweet and romantic to me. I enjoyed his arms around me because I knew I would never have them around me again. It was hard to say I no longer loved him. He had been my everything for so long that it was hard to completely stop loving him, but he had to be punished. I waited until he fell fast asleep then snuck out of the house for the special ingredient I needed for Thanksgiving dinner. It took me a little bit of effort but eventually, I got what I needed. Back at home I quickly began to make the provisions to the turkey with the secret ingredient. I peeked at Kris and was happy to see he was still sound asleep.

I crushed up some sleeping pills and carefully put them into the peach tea I made special. Kris loved peach tea, and I had made it a habit to make him it every holiday. I had to add more peaches to mask the bitter taste of the sleeping pills. Everything was ready, now it was time to grab a couple of hours of sleep before the best Thanksgiving dinner ever. I fell asleep with a smile on my face. Kris woke up and we began our tradition of Thanksgiving. We spent the morning talking and laughing as we prepared food. While

I was working on a crossword I always did on Thanksgiving, Kris was enjoying his first glass of homemade peach tea. By the time, I had finished my crossword, Kris was snoring on the couch with the glass still in his hand. Smiling I took the glass and dumped the contents down the sink. I carefully washed the glass and then did the same with the entire pitcher of peach tea I made.

I made sure everything was washed, and I dumped the rest of the sleeping pills down the toilet. I got rid of the pill bottle in the neighbor's trash after I took the label off. I began to lay out the food on the kitchen table, and then I dragged Kris's sleeping body to a chair. I didn't have anything to subdue him that wouldn't leave any marks so I just propped him up in his favorite chair. It was time. It was time to wake Kris. I put several five-hour energy shots into a syringe and injected them into the back of his head where I knew he had a mole. I was careful to make sure that everything had been disposed of. I sat back down at the table as he began to wake up. "You fell asleep." I laughed as Kris looked around confused. He grinned at me sheepishly as he began to fix himself a big Thanksgiving plate.

"I changed the recipe this year on the turkey. I hope you like it. I wanted it to be spicier." I said as I offered him a huge helping of turkey. He nodded and began to eat. "Wow, this is the best turkey you have ever made Crystal! I am impressed." He was grinning from ear to ear. "Please, have some more turkey." I offered him the plate. He ate almost the entire turkey to himself in less than forty-five minutes. "Do you like the new recipe?" I asked with my eyes shining with happiness. "Yes! What did you do to it?" He asked patting his stomach happily. I began to clear the dishes with a smile on my face. "How about some desert?" I offered him a plate of cheesecake I made by hand. "It's cherry cheesecake." I offered a smile.

He happily began to eat the cheesecake. "This is amazing." He was eating like he hadn't eaten in months. Before I got the rest of the dishes put up and cleaned he had eaten the entire cheesecake. "Where did you learn to cook like that?" He asked in amazement. I sat back down at the kitchen table with my hands under my chin. "I'll tell you a secret." I giggled. I was ready to tell him what I had done.

"Do you know your mistress, Annabell? The one you have been seeing for what seems like a year and six months?" I paused watching his face go pale. "Well, after I found out you had taken all my money, I paid her a special visit. That turkey was not just turkey but it was stuffed with spices and her. I killed her and used her body as stuffing for the turkey. The cherry on the cheesecake was her blood mixed with sugar. The best part is, you ate her entire body except for her bones and teeth." I paused again watching Kris's reaction to my words.

"You... did.... What?" He whispered. "Don't worry love, I made sure to frame you for her murder." I laughed. From a far away distance, I could hear sirens. "Just in time!" Kris tried to stand up but found himself not moving. The cheesecake had a temporary paralytic drug so he wouldn't run. "Oh, it's time for my performance." I smiled sweetly at Kris. I took his hand and wrapped his hand around the hilt of the knife. "I hope she was worth everything you ruined," I whispered to him as I rammed his hand holding the knife into my stomach. Gasping at the pain, I made him stab me once more. He was still holding the knife thanks to the drugs in his system. I fell to the floor holding my stomach. The cops began to knock at the door. Eventually, they came in right as the paralytic drugs began to wear off. Kris stood up, covered in my blood still holding the knife. Kris got tased by the police as he was insisting I was the true killer. Everything began to feel cold, as I slipped into darkness. I could hear paramedics coming into my place as they tried to save my life.

I spent about a month in the hospital playing the part of the frightened wife. I gave my statement to the cops about how that Thanksgiving dinner Kris went crazy. When I got out of the hospital, I found that people were more than generous with donations. Everyone felt so sorry for me. Annabell was found, and the evidence pointed to Kris.

Kris's trial happened within a few months. He was found guilty of first-degree murder and attempted murder. He was found guilty of embezzlement and fraud because the bank gave my statements to the court. Life with no chance of parole was what he got. I hired the best attorney I could find, and was able to file for divorce. Kris sent me letters for the first year he was in prison, but I sent them all back unopened. I was able to sell my house and his car. Soon, my financial situation was back to where I had it before he decided to take the money out. By next Thanksgiving, I was in a new state, with a new man and life was great again. But that's the thing about happiness and love. You only see what you want to see. Behind that illusion lies deadly secrets.

"I think this year, I am going to do a spicy turkey for dinner." I smiled at my new husband, Clint. "Sure honey, whatever you want." He said absentmindedly as he played on his phone. It was going to be another Thanksgiving to remember.

The End

About the author: Allisha McAdoo started writing at a very young age and fell in love with writing horror. She was first published in 2017 and continues to release more each year. She currently has 53 books published on Amazon, Google Play,

Apple Books, Nook, Kobo, Kindle, Goodreads, Smashwords, Pubshare, and Godless. With no plans of stopping writing look forward for more coming soon.

Author's note

Did you enjoy this Thanksgiving Anthology? I hope so, I picked as many twisted stories as I could. :) I hope you read each story while eating Thanksgiving dinner. Stay tuned for more works from all these fantastic authors!

THE END!

Made in the USA
Columbia, SC
23 November 2023